FENELLA J. MILLER

◆

A MOST DELIGHTFUL CHRISTMAS

Complete and Unabridged

LINFORD
Leicester

First published in Great Britain in 2019

First Linford Edition
published 2019

A catalogue record for this book is available
from the British Library.

ISBN 978–1–4448–4167–1

Published by
F. A. Thorpe (Publishing)
Anstey, Leicestershire

Set by Words & Graphics Ltd.
Anstey, Leicestershire
Printed and bound in Great Britain by
T. J. International Ltd., Padstow, Cornwall

This book is printed on acid-free paper

1

Finchley Hall, November.

'Have you run mad, Abingdon? What you are suggesting is quite preposterous, and I cannot let you undertake such a ridiculous scheme.' Richard thumped the table to make his point. 'I am next in line to your title and should be allowed a say in the matter. You must let me bail you out and pay your debtors; it's the least I can do for you.'

His cousin, Lord Sylvester Finchley, Earl of Abingdon, viewed him with disfavour. 'I am determined to go ahead, whatever you say to the contrary. You have no interest in becoming an aristocrat, as you much prefer to be plain Mr Richard Finchley, and by doing this I will ensure you do not have to do something you don't want.' He downed a second, or possibly a third, glass of brandy before continuing.

'You have been coming to my rescue too often, my friend. This dismal state of affairs is entirely my own fault, and I must face up to my responsibilities. I have already sent instructions to my lawyers, and the letters will go out tomorrow or the next day.'

'I cannot believe you intend to auction yourself to the highest bidder — you could be obliged to marry someone totally unsuitable. At least agree that you will meet a selection of the candidates before you make your choice.'

'Abingdon Manor is in a sad state of disrepair; only your continued generosity has kept my mother and sisters from being destitute. I shall be forever grateful that you offered them a home with your mama, as they would have fared far worse if they had remained with me.'

'I am very fond of your family, and they are ideal companionship for my mother. I shall hold a Christmas house party at Finchley Hall, and then we can invite the highest bidders for your hand and title.'

'Are you sure this will not be too much of an imposition? I cannot guarantee that those who are invited will be convivial company. They will be gentlemen who have made their fortune in trade and wish to gain entry to the *ton* by marrying a daughter to me. I might be impoverished, but my line goes back unbroken for centuries. It is unfortunate that the majority of the holders of this prestigious title have been inveterate gamblers, and even an estate as large as mine cannot support such deprivations.'

'At least you have not sold any land; your estates are intact even if your pockets are to let.' Richard poured himself a stiff drink. 'I suppose there is little difference in you being auctioned and what each Season's debutantes have to endure. After all, are they not paraded around Almack's like broodmares in a sale ring for the gentlemen to decide which one they would wish to ride?'

'I had never thought of it like that. And I accept your kind offer to host a house party in my honour. How many of the suitable candidates should I invite? Do you intend to have any of your friends and acquaintances come too?'

'I think it would be the height of folly to have only the highest bidders there. I shall make sure there are as many ordinary guests, as there are those wishing to ensnare an earl for their daughter.' Richard could not prevent a yawn escaping and tried to cover it by coughing. It was well past midnight, and his estate manager was coming for a meeting before breakfast tomorrow.

'I'm going to retire, Abingdon. You may stay here and drink yourself into a stupor if you so wish. I shall speak to my mother tomorrow about the arrangements. I can't remember the last time we had guests over the Christmas period, and it will make a pleasant change to have the house full.'

'By the by, I don't want my mother or sisters to know what I am about. Give me your word you will not reveal my secret.'

'I doubt that it will remain secret for long, as one or other of the guests is bound to mention it. Also, how am I to explain to my mother, and your aunt, that I have suddenly taken it into my head to hold a house party, and half those I am inviting are complete strangers to us all?'

Abingdon waved an empty glass in his direction. 'You are a clever fellow. You will think of a way of bringing this about.'

He left his cousin slumped over the decanter and made his way to his apartment. He had always thought it ironic that in every case the second son, the one who did not inherit, would have been the better candidate than the eldest. It hardly seemed credible that over the centuries this pattern had been repeated time after time.

His father, Lord David Finchley, had been an astute businessman as well as an excellent landlord, and on his demise five years ago he had left the estates in good heart and the coffers brimming. Mama was frequently telling Richard that at the age of eight and twenty he should be thinking about becoming leg-shackled himself. Having only had the one child, himself, she was eager to fill the house with grandchildren she could dote on.

He was in no hurry to set up his nursery, but understood it was something he should be considering in the next year or two. However, he would first get his cousin safely married to the least appalling of the candidates.

* * *

The following day, Richard joined his parent for breakfast and was pleased to see that his aunt and cousins were also there. 'Good morning, ladies. There is something I wish to discuss with you.'

He had their full attention. He was not famous for discussing anything with anyone. He, like his deceased father, made up his own mind without speaking of his plans.

'I have decided to open the house for a Christmas house party. I need a list of those families you wish to include, Mama, and please feel free to add some with marriageable daughters.'

The older ladies exchanged glances whilst his cousins just smiled happily.

'Abingdon has asked his lawyers to supply a list of heiresses so he may choose himself a suitable bride. I shall leave the details to the pair of you. I think the invitations must go out by the end of the week, as we are already into November.'

Halston Court, December.

'I do not wish to accompany you to this house party, Mama. You must take Lucy instead. I shall do perfectly well here on my own, taking care of my horses and my dogs.'

'You shall do no such thing, Frederica Halston. You are the eldest, and your papa is prepared to pay a fortune in order to make you a countess.'

'My sister is far prettier than me, and I'm certain that his lordship would much prefer her for a wife. I am too plain, too forthright, and have no interest whatsoever in becoming the wife of an aristocrat. Indeed, no interest in becoming anybody's wife.'

Her mother drew breath for another tirade but was interrupted by the arrival of Papa.

'There you are, my dear Freddie. I see that your mother has given you the good news. It will be a most delightful Christmas, and I cannot wait to visit Finchley Hall and rub shoulders with some of the most important families in the country.'

'Papa, did you specify which daughter you wanted to marry the earl?'

'No, I just put in my bid and received

the invitation to attend this festive gathering so his lordship can make his choice. I expect there to be half a dozen other hopeful young ladies and their parents present, as well as the friends and acquaintances of the Finchley family.'

'In which case, it would make more sense for Lucy to be put forward in my stead. It can make little difference to you which daughter is a countess as you will still have gained entry to the drawing rooms of the *ton*.'

Her sister had been listening to this exchange with interest. 'Am I not to be asked if I wish to be married to a complete stranger and obliged to live in a draughty old house?'

'I shall ask you now, my dear Lucy. Would you prefer to be a countess, or would you wish your sister to take that position?'

Lucy pouted and put her finger on her lips as if she were an empty-headed young lady. She was, in fact, highly intelligent and an equal on every level to her sister. 'I think on balance, I will volunteer to sacrifice myself for the good of the family. No doubt the vast amount of money you are paying, Papa, will mean that my future husband can modernise our home and remove the draughts.'

Their mama did not seem so sanguine about this change of plans. 'I cannot allow my youngest daughter to be married before my oldest — it will not do, Mr Halston, it will not do at all. If Frederica can find herself a different husband, then you may put Lucy forward, otherwise we shall continue as before.'

Freddie exchanged a worried glance with her sister, who immediately rose to the occasion.

'Mama, if there are to be other girls from whom the earl can choose, then he will not select Freddie. I, on the other hand, am fashionably fair, have periwinkle-blue eyes, curves in all the correct places, and am neither too petite nor too tall.'

'Whereas I, on the other hand, am none of those things. As you are both so set on having an aristocrat in the family, then I should think you would want to put forward the most likely option.' Freddie held her breath, and after a few moments' cogitation her mother nodded.

'Very well, but do not think, young lady, that this means you can remain behind. Your papa has not spent a fortune on your new wardrobe for it to languish in your closet and never be seen.'

'Then the matter is settled, Mrs Halston, and there need be no further discussion on the subject.' He waved the gold-embossed card around like a trophy. 'It states on here that we are to arrive five days before Christmas Day itself. We will have to stop twice on the journey, so that means we must leave here next week if we are not to be tardy.'

Freddie and her sister escaped from the drawing room through one door as their papa vanished through another, leaving their mama to summon the housekeeper in order to convey this information.

'That went perfectly, Lucy. I don't know why we didn't think of this before.'

'I never thought our family would be selected — I wonder how much papa had to offer in order to get on the invitation list?' Her sister frowned. 'What if this man I am to marry is a gambler and drunkard? How will that help advance our parents in society?'

'I heard our parents discussing this very matter a week or two ago. Papa was most insistent that he had checked the credentials of the earl; although he comes from a long line of gamblers, he is not one himself. Anyway, our grandfather came back so rich from his travels to India that I doubt even the most profligate of husbands could ever hope to spend it in one lifetime.'

'We have yet to examine the boxes of gowns, undergarments, gloves, shoes and other bits and pieces that arrived yesterday. Shall we see if our choices look as good in reality as they did on the fashion plates?' Lucy said.

'All I can say is that I am heartily thankful our mother was absent on the day the seamstress came to take our measurements. If she had been able to interfere, we would both be dressed like maypoles, every gown festooned from top to bottom with rouleaux, ribbons and gold buttons.'

'Also, Freddie, each gown would be a pale colour — if coloured at all. She wishes us both to look exactly like all the other hopeful young debutantes. I think we will cause somewhat of a stir at this house party when we appear in our new ensembles.'

'Then I think it would be wise, sister dearest, if we keep our mother away from our new garments until it is too late for her to change anything.' Freddie heard the crunch of carriage wheels on the turning circle outside. 'Quickly; we shall be obliged to make insipid conversation with any morning callers if we remain here much longer.'

She slipped her arm through her sister's and together they scampered upstairs. She continued to the nursery floor, where she had her studio and her beloved spaniels awaited her. When she entered, three furry bodies roused themselves from their position on the rag rug in front of the roaring fire. She dropped to her knees and they climbed all over her, barking and licking in excitement because she had returned.

'Silly boys. I have only been gone an hour or two. I'm going to finish my painting whilst there is still light enough, and then I will put on my boots and take you for another walk.'

★　★　★

Richard followed his mother around the house, doing his best to sound enthusiastic at the suggestions she was making.

'The yule log must be fetched in on Christmas Eve; it is the traditional way to do it. We have never followed the old ways here, and I cannot tell you how excited I am to think this house will be decked out with holly, ivy, mistletoe and other greenery, as well as ribbons, candles and baubles. The place will look magnificent and must impress our guests.'

'I'm sure it will look lovely, Mama. I'm looking forward to seeing it decorated. There will be more than fifty people, plus their personal servants, staying here, and a further fifty will attend the ball on Twelfth Night. Are you sure that everything is in hand to feed so many?'

'Bevan has it well in hand, my dear; you can be very sure no one will go hungry. Two dozen extra inside staff have been taken on for the festive period, as well as a dozen extra grooms. Adequate accommodation has been prepared for the visiting servants, and in the past week extra supplies have been coming from all over the country.'

'Then it is fortunate indeed, Mama, that I have deep pockets. From the flurry of visiting modistes, I take it you are in the process of replenishing your wardrobes?'

'You hardly need to ask such a thing, my dear. You can be very sure we will all be in the first stare of fashion and not let any parvenus, cits or anyone else outshine the ladies of the family. I am assuming that you and Abingdon will be suitably attired?'

'Am I not always the epitome of sartorial elegance?' He helped himself from the chafing dishes set over the hot water and took his piled plate to his usual place at the end of the table.

Richard had grave doubts about the outcome of this enterprise, but intended to do everything he could to help his cousin find himself an heiress who wasn't too far beyond the pale. He rather thought it wouldn't be the lady who was the problem but her parents, who might well be quite impossible.

Over the past weeks, the house had been cleaned from top to bottom, and he was heartily sick of dodging busy servants wielding dusters and mops. The weather was appalling — torrential rain, howling gales; and if it didn't improve, he doubted any of the guests, apart from those who lived in the vicinity, would be able to come.

Cartloads of greenery had been fetched from the woods, and this was now being formed into wreaths, garlands and suchlike which were going to be festooned about the place. The ladies of his household had been busy making bows from ribbon, and Richard was informed that Cook had baked dozens of biscuits which were to be hung up as well. He sincerely hoped having food left around the place would not encourage rodents to come in.

* * *

Three days before the first guests were expected to arrive, Richard got up to find there had been a hard frost and everywhere was sparkling in the sunlight. The roads would be rutted, but at least they would now be passable.

Abingdon had arrived the previous day and seemed resigned rather than excited about the next few weeks. 'The more I think about it, the less I like the idea of buying my bride. I wish I had never thought of this scheme.'

'It is too late to repine, my friend. You are committed now. Although you have gone about this in an unconventional manner, you're doing no more than hundreds of gentlemen before you. You are marrying to restore your fortunes and protect your inheritance. The woman you select will become a countess and be a member of the ruling classes.'

'That's all very well, but I would much prefer to marry someone I had feelings for.'

'You will have several young ladies to choose from — there must be one at least amongst them who appeals to you. As long as you are happy to share your bed with the woman you select, then I can hardly see it matters if you do not have romantic feelings for her.'

'Unlike you, cousin, I had always thought I would fall in love with a beautiful woman . . . '

'It is a damn good thing you didn't, for she was bound to be someone unsuitable and impoverished. I can remember at least three occasions when you declared yourself in love, and each of the young ladies concerned were from the lower classes. If I hadn't stepped in to extricate you, you would now be married to a serving wench and your estates would belong to the bank.'

Abingdon was forced to smile. 'You are correct to remind me of my folly. I shall choose the prettiest lady; then at least we will have attractive children together.'

'I think it would be more sensible to look at the parents before you make your decision. The daughter of the least undesirable of the families should be your choice. If you find that an unpalatable suggestion, then allow me to do that for you.'

'That would be capital. I thank you; I shall get to know the young ladies but leave you to make the selection for me.'

Their conversation was interrupted as a dozen outdoor men staggered in with an enormous log scattering debris and mud in all directions. Richard was about to roar at them when he hesitated. It wasn't their fault that his parent wished to have this tree trunk burning in the fireplace in the entrance hall.

'Shall we escape to the billiard room? I think the house will be in chaos whilst our mothers have the decorations placed. I thought these should not go up until the day before Christmas, but I suppose it makes sense to have the house decorated before the guests arrive.'

2

'Freddie, I think we are about to turn down the drive of Finchley Hall. I wish the house party was being held where I would be living if I were selected.' Lucy pointed out of the window, and she was right — they were approaching an elegant entrance flanked by two gate-houses.

As the coachman slowed to enter, her mother roused from her slumber. There had been blessed silence for the past three hours as both parents had been asleep.

'Mr Halston, wake up do; we are almost there. If this is the home of the cousin, then Abingdon Manor must be magnificent indeed.'

Her father slowly sat up, yawned, and rubbed his eyes. 'My enquiries say that the house and estates of the earl are in a sad state of repair. This is the reason he must marry money. I shall insist on being involved in the restorations, as it will be my money that pays for them.'

Freddie exchanged a glance with her sister. This did not bode well. No aristocrat would brook any interference from a commoner. Then she realised that this was exactly what they wanted. Lucy did not really wish to marry for any other reason than love, but as dutiful daughters, they would do as they were bid. However, if somehow his lordship could take a dislike to her parents, then it would not be Lucy's fault if she was not selected.

She widened her eyes and nodded towards her father. Her sister understood immediately, and for the first time in several weeks her smile was genuine. They would, no doubt, be sharing a bedchamber and have plenty of time to plan their strategy. They could not misbehave themselves, but they would take every opportunity to show their parents in the worst possible light.

Her father was second-generation money, had had an excellent education and married the youngest daughter of a lord — the fact that this gentleman was an impoverished Irish lord made no difference. He had made a small step in the right direction and was now determined to gain entry to the best drawing rooms in the country by marrying Lucy into the Finchley dynasty.

He could not have a title for himself, but gaining one for his daughter would be the next best thing as far as he was concerned. Freddie's parents appeared either unaware or unconcerned they would still be considered beneath the touch of a true aristocratic family. She had no time for such nonsense herself. Whilst not exactly a republican, she certainly believed wealth should be distributed more evenly and that power should not remain solely in the hands of the aristocracy.

Her allowance, which was more than enough for a family to live on in comfort, was spent mainly on charitable ventures; and there were many who owed, if not their lives, then their health and livelihood to her good offices. Her mother knew nothing about this — she would have put a stop to it at once — but her father was aware of how she spent her pin money, and if not exactly approving, he did nothing to prevent her. He was a good man at heart; the villages within his estate, the farms and those that he employed, had nothing to complain of. They were all fairly paid and treated well.

Mama was respected and popular with her peers, but as none of them had blue blood running through their veins, they were not enough. She was determined to be able to count lords and ladies in her circle of friends.

Whatever happened over the festive period, at least Freddie's parents would have had their dearest wish and have been able to mingle with those they most admired. She sent up a quick prayer to the Lord Almighty that those they aspired to be like would not give them the cut direct.

'It is a magnificent house, Mr Halston. I believe it to be as large as our own establishment.'

'It is considerably older than ours, but a handsome building nonetheless. Well, ladies, put on your bonnets and gloves, as we will be arriving in a few minutes. There is another vehicle behind us, but I believe we might be the first.'

When the carriage rocked to a standstill, everything was in place: bonnet ribbons tied, gloves smoothed carefully over fingers, and creases in gowns shaken out. Two footmen in half-wigs and smart bottle-green livery had the door open and the steps lowered in an instant. They handed their mother down as if she were royalty.

Papa should have waited for Freddie and Lucy to disembark, but he followed, leaving them alone for a few precious moments. 'I am dreading this, Freddie, but at least we can hide away together if needs be.'

'I think it is fortunate we had the best dance masters and tutors, so we can be sure we are as well-educated and proficient as any other young lady at this house party. Our gowns have come from the most expensive mantua-maker in town, so we can hold our heads high without fear of looking provincial.'

Freddie knew better than to interact with a servant, so accepted the gloved hand that was offered without making eye contact. Their parents were already at the door being bowed in by two individuals; the gentleman in the black frock coat she assumed was the butler, the woman in grey bombazine the housekeeper.

They were obliged to pick up their skirts and run if they were not to be left outside. Whatever the senior members of staff had said, Freddie and her sister were too late to hear it. She stopped so abruptly her sister almost lost her footing.

'Look at that — doesn't it look beautiful? Imagine how it will be when the candles that are pushed into the garlands are lit this evening.'

'See, Freddie, there is a kissing bough hanging in the centre. Everywhere I look, there is something else to enjoy. I'm beginning to think that this Christmas visit might be more enjoyable than we anticipated.'

'Quickly — we must follow. There will be time to examine the decorations later on.' Freddie was determined not to be left marooned in the hall.

A footman was conducting her parents up the magnificent marble staircase that dominated the entrance space. The steps were so wide that there was ample room for a small potted tree to be placed on either side. Each one was decorated and added to the general festive feeling of the house.

'I suppose we just follow on behind, Lucy. We can hardly linger here, as there is another family close behind.'

The substantial gallery at the head of the staircase had three passageways leading from it. Freddie's parents were escorted to the left, and the footman stopped in front of a door and opened it with a flourish. 'This is your apartment, sir, madam. Your valet and dresser have already unpacked your trunks.' He bowed and then turned. 'If you would care to follow me, Miss Halston, Miss Lucy, you have an apartment at the rear of the house overlooking the garden.'

After a considerable walk, they arrived at their destination, and Freddie was happy with their accommodation. Mary and Polly, their maids, were waiting to greet them.

'It's ever so nice here, miss, and we've got a room next door and don't have to sleep in the attics,' Mary said. One could always rely on one's maid to fill in the details. 'You have a bedchamber each but you share this parlour.'

The room was well appointed with all the necessary furniture, including a desk, a well-filled bookcase, a chaise longue and two comfortable armchairs grouped invitingly in front of a substantial fire.

'Are we the first to arrive, Mary?'

'No, Miss Lucy; another family came an hour or so ago. The young ladies are to be together in this wing and the young gentlemen will be on the other side of the house. The married couples have the more substantial apartments to the left and right of the family wing.'

'Thank you, Mary. We should like to change from our travelling clothes into something more suitable. I take it there is hot water available?'

Polly giggled and pointed to a doorway that led from the dressing room they were standing in. 'You won't believe your eyes, miss, when you look in there.'

This room was a special chamber devoted entirely to bathing. A large bath stood in the centre of the room with one end adjacent to the wall. 'This is quite extraordinary; even we do not have such a place at home,' her sister explained. 'See, Freddie, there is a special plug to go in this aperture, and I believe that when it is removed the water exits on its own.'

'Extraordinary indeed — think how much easier it makes the life of the chambermaids. I wonder, do all the apartments have one of these?'

'No, miss; I think you are the only young ladies to have one. Mr and Mrs Halston have one also, and I gather there are others available for the family, but not for the guests,' Polly said.

It was impossible to continue this discussion whilst their maids were present; but as soon as they were alone, Freddie returned to the subject.

'You know what this means don't you, Lucy? Our family has been singled out for preferential treatment — I think Papa must be the highest bidder, or possibly the least objectionable of the candidates.'

'I thought exactly the same thing. Mama will be in high alt as soon as she is aware we are the only family to have our own bathing rooms. This is going to make our task so much more difficult.'

Freddie's sister, although very like

herself in many respects, did not have the resilience that she had, and would give in to difficult circumstances rather than continue fighting. 'You must not worry about it, dearest. Leave the matter to me. All *you* have to do is behave as our parents expect. I shall come up with some stratagems once I have met all the families in contention and also the gentleman himself.'

They had lingered here long enough and must go down and make their curtsies.

'Although the house party is being held for Lord Finchley, I suppose Mr Finchley and his mother are the actual host and hostess of this event. The dowager countess and the earl take precedence of rank, but . . . '

'There is no point in worrying about it, Freddie, we shall discover for ourselves as soon as we go down. I think that ensemble you have chosen is perfect on you. Duck-egg blue is an unusual colour, and not every young lady could carry it off.'

'Your primrose gown with that gold sash and the beading around the neckline and hem will be the envy of every other young lady here. I just hope that our mother does not create a scene when she sees us wearing colours and not white.'

Arm in arm they retraced their steps, crossed the impressive gallery, and made their way down the marble staircase. They were greeted by none other than the butler himself.

'Foster at your service, Miss Halston, Miss Lucy. If you would care to make your way into the drawing room, there are refreshments being served.'

His polite instructions were unnecessary, as the double doors to this chamber were open and the sound of voices carried into the vast entrance hall. Lucy tensed and Freddie squeezed her hand.

'It will be fine, Lucy. We must forget why we have been invited here and just enjoy ourselves.'

Richard had been observing the arrivals from the safety of his study. He had no intention of mingling with these people until he had no option but to do so. The highest bidders would arrive today, and those he wished to spend time with would be arriving tomorrow. Abingdon wanted to assess each candidate before the house party became too busy.

The first carriage disgorged what one might expect from a gentleman, if one might call him so, who was prepared to buy his daughter a husband. The older woman had a voice so strident one could hear every word she said even from this distance. The husband emerged last and seemed a decent sort of fellow. The daughter was a younger, quieter replica of her mother, and the young man he must suppose was the heir to the shipping empire his father controlled.

He returned to his perusal of the pile of business correspondence that had arrived that morning, but put it aside when he heard the crunch of carriage wheels an hour or so later. He returned to his vantage point where he could see but not be seen himself.

The first to descend from the luxurious vehicle was a tall, elegant woman who held herself proudly and could have been mistaken for one of the family's acquaintances. To his surprise, instead of the young ladies stepping down, the father did so. This was bad form — ladies always came first. He dismissed this gentleman and waited to see what the daughter was like.

A tall, slender young woman emerged first, the image of her mother. It was hard to see her face beneath the wide brim of her fashionable bonnet. However, he was immediately aware that they were as different as chalk from cheese to the first family that had arrived. A second young lady descended; she was shorter than the first, but equally well-dressed. Again, her features were hidden from him.

He watched them hurry after their

parents and was intrigued to know more about this family. The list of those invited was on his desk and he examined it. Yes — these must be the Halstons. They were second-generation money and were not so far beyond the pale as to be totally unacceptable.

The second paper he perused set out where each family would be staying during their three-week visit. He had been right in his assumption — this family had been given the best accommodation, so Abingdon must also think that one of the daughters was the most likely candidate.

One must presume that the taller woman, Miss Frederica Halston, was the oldest, and the other was Miss Lucy. It would be interesting to examine both more closely and decide which one would be most suitable as the next Countess of Abingdon.

He remained incommunicado until he was obliged to return to his apartment and change for dinner. There would be thirty-eight at the table tonight, and he was almost looking forward to seeing the grand dining room in use for the first time since his father had died five years ago.

As Richard was about to leave his apartment, his cousin burst in without knocking — an irritating habit which never failed to annoy him.

'They are all here, and I wish them to perdition already. This was a bad idea, and you should have stopped me from doing it.'

'Too late to repine, my friend. You are committed to this enterprise. There is one family that might do — the Halstons — so do not despair. If you find no one to your liking, then you will allow me to settle your debts and restore your estates. This is not a request. This is how it will be.'

Richard's cousin raised his hands. 'Very well, I agree. I am not happy about it, but beggars cannot be choosers.'

The racket from the drawing room indicated many of the guests were already downstairs, no doubt being plied with champagne or sherry wine.

'Courage, Abingdon. You must not flinch, or indicate by the slightest gesture that you have a preference for one girl over another.'

'Why not? Surely if I make a speedy choice, if I make one at all, it will mean the house party is more enjoyable for everyone here? The unsuccessful families can then relax and enjoy your lavish hospitality.'

'They could also behave badly and turn my house into a shambles. I'll not have you risk it, cousin. We will stick to the plan, and you must not reveal your choice until the night of the ball when they will all be departing the next day.'

As always, Abingdon acquiesced with a smile. 'I rely on your good sense and judgement, and shall do as you say.' He paused just out of sight of those occupying the drawing room. 'God's teeth! It sounds like a bear garden in there. Are you ready for this?'

Richard stepped aside and allowed

his cousin to walk in first. From his relaxed stance, one would never have known Abingdon was nervous.

The sound of feminine laughter on the stairs made him glance over his shoulder. It was the Halston girls. He caught his breath and could not take his eyes from them. The younger girl, Miss Lucy, was a diamond of the first water. She had golden curls, startlingly blue eyes and a perfect figure. He scarcely looked at the sister, although she too was elegantly gowned and passably attractive.

3

Freddie whispered into her sister's ear, 'The tall gentleman with hair the colour of a raven's wing must be Mr Finchley. He is staring at you in a most particular manner. I think his cousin has acquired a rival for your affections.' Her comment was intended to be humorous, but Lucy shivered.

'He is not at all the sort of gentleman I would wish to be pursued by — too fierce-looking and far too tall. I do hope you are incorrect.'

'Don't fret about it, dearest. Remember I intend to make us both *persona non grata* long before the end of this house party. I promise you neither of them will wish to marry you, and you will be free to return home after the ball.'

The gentleman in question had not waited to introduce himself but continued his progress into the drawing room.

The space was huge, and even with so many people milling about, there was still room for dozens more. As soon as they stepped inside, a footman offered them a glass of champagne on a silver tray.

Freddie shook her head and waved him away. Alcohol did not agree with Lucy, and she herself wished to keep a clear head tonight.

As they paused in the open doorway, she became uncomfortably aware they were the centre of attention. Her sister was by far the loveliest young lady in the room, and the other guests were obviously assessing her potential. If it was generally known that the Halston family had been given the best accommodation, everyone would know that Lucy was the front runner in this bizarre race.

An elegant lady with fading blonde hair and a burgundy silk evening gown approached with a friendly smile. 'Good evening, my dears. I am the dowager countess and would like to welcome you to Finchley Hall.'

They both curtsied and responded as expected. Freddie waited for her ladyship to take them around the chamber and introduce them to the other guests, but this didn't happen.

'Dinner is about to be served. We were just waiting for you to join us.'

For anyone else, this would have been a disastrous start, but Freddie seized the opportunity to further alienate their hostess.

'I do beg your pardon, my lady, if we are tardy. Mama has always told us that it is better to arrive last; then we ourselves will not be kept waiting by other guests.' This was a shocking thing to say, and her ladyship's expression changed to frosty. With a disdainful nod, the dowager countess turned her back and sailed across to talk to someone less impolite.

Lucy glanced up at her and half-smiled. 'Mama will be mortified if she hears what you said, but your plan is already working.'

'I am a little uneasy about having been so impertinent, as we both gave our word that we would not misbehave, and what I just did was certainly not the behaviour of a well-brought-up young lady.'

'Fiddlesticks to that! I think it highly unlikely that our parents will ever get to hear about your misdemeanour, Freddie, and we must ensure we are impeccably behaved when they are there to observe. I believe you will be able to give the earl a disgust of both of us, and he will move on to one of the other families for his choice.'

The butler announced that dinner was served, and there was a general push towards the door. It appeared guests did not have to process in order of precedence, but made their way in and found their seats themselves.

As they had come in last, Freddie and Lucy were at the end of the line. When they eventually reached the dining room, it was to discover there were only two chairs empty and they were not together. 'Lucy, you take the seat next to the young lady in pink flounces, and I will take the other one.'

Her sister was gone immediately, which did not surprise Freddie, as the other vacant place was next to Mr Finchley. A footman politely pulled out the chair, and she slipped into the seat without making eye contact with anyone around her.

Disapproval radiated from the gentleman on her right. From his demeanour, she was sure he had overheard her remark to his aunt, and held her in contempt. The earl was sitting next to a young lady who looked so like him she must be one of his three sisters. On his other side was an older woman who she thought might be the parent of the gentleman next to her.

The first course was served *á la française*, which meant the removes were placed centrally down the table and the guests left to help themselves from whatever took their fancy. It was customary for a gentleman to serve the ladies on either side of him, and Freddie waited to see if the man next to her would do so or leave her with an empty plate.

'Miss Halston, what would you like?'

She risked a glance at him and regretted it. He was doing what was expected of him, but his jaw was hard and his eyes arctic. Freddie had intended to smile prettily and behave with decorum, but something about his arrogance made her do the reverse.

'I am quite capable of choosing for myself, sir. You have no wish to serve me, and I have no wish to be served by you.'

Without waiting for him to give her a set-down, she followed her words with actions. Fortunately, she had longer arms than most young ladies and could reach easily to the centre of the table. She helped herself to a random selection of items and then picked up her cutlery and prepared to begin her meal. The things she had chosen were so smothered in rich cream sauces that she had no idea what she was eating. She had taken no more than a few mouthfuls when, to her surprise, he addressed her a second time. 'I hope, Miss Halston, that you are fond of fish, as everything you have taken is from the sea.'

She forgot her dislike of this man and couldn't stop her squeak of distress. 'I am allergic to seafood. I must go, as I shall be horribly ill at any moment.'

She shoved back her chair so hard it tumbled over, and she was for the second time the centre of disapproving glances. With a napkin held over her mouth, she fled the room but had no idea in which direction to go.

Then someone was beside her, a strong arm was about her waist, and she was whisked across the drawing room and out onto the terrace not a moment too soon. She made the balustrade and then cast up her accounts. When she was done, she wiped her mouth on her napkin and pressed her knees against the stonework in an effort to hold herself upright.

A warm jacket was draped around

her shoulders. 'Are you able to walk, my dear, or do you wish me to carry you back to your apartment? I take it you do not wish to return to the dining room.'

'I do not. Thank you, Mr Finchley, for your timely assistance. It serves me right for being so rude to you. I am recovered now and can find my own way.'

She slipped the jacket off and held it out. 'Thank you again, sir, and I do hope I have not ruined your dinner by my . . . '

'I think the least said about that the better. I will make your apologies. Before you go, Miss Halston, is there anything else that you are allergic to? I shall make sure my chef prepares you a special diet that does not make you ill.'

'Only fish, I thank the Lord. Please return to the table; I shall remain out here for a while longer and enjoy the fresh air before returning to my apartment.'

He nodded politely and strolled off.

For any other young lady, this would have been an unmitigated disaster; but being so very unwell would only add to his dislike of her. Although, if she were honest, he had been remarkably kind despite her impertinence.

★   ★   ★

Richard returned to the dinner table with rather less enthusiasm than he had initially. As he was about to resume his place, he became aware he was being stared at from further down the table. The younger sister looked upset.

He walked around until he was directly behind her. 'Your sister unfortunately ate some fish. She is well now and has retired.'

'Oh dear! How horrid for both of you. Thank you so much for taking care of her.' She smiled and looked even more enchanting if that were possible.

'It was my absolute pleasure, Miss Lucy.' He did not wish to show his partiality and thus raise the suspicions of the tabbies watching this exchange with interest, so he nodded and returned to his side of the table.

He ate sparingly, for some reason finding the rich food unpalatable. His French chef was the envy of his neighbours, and until this evening he had not thought much about what was set out in front of him each night. He expected to have the best staff available, and had appointed this emigre because the man had come with such an impressive reputation.

If everything served was not so disguised with sauce, Miss Halston would have been able to recognise what she was about to eat and leave it on her plate. He would speak to his mother tomorrow and in future would demand that plainer food be served. Lord Tewkesbury had been trying to entice the Frenchman away, and he would allow the chef to leave his employ. From now on, the kitchen would prepare the wholesome British food that had always been served in this house until a year ago.

Richard was obliged to make conversation with the matron sitting on his right, and discovered that she was a Mrs Huntingdon-Smyth married to a gentleman who had made a vast fortune with his manufactories in the north of England. She was a garrulous woman, not overly bright, and certainly not someone he would wish to welcome into the family.

When his mother stood up, the other ladies followed, and he was left with his cousin and the gentlemen to drink port and talk of matters that were not suitable for feminine ears. He listened with interest to Mr Halston discuss at great length the problems enclosure had caused, and the man made it plain that he had sympathy for those who could no longer keep their own livestock, pigs, or farm a strip of land for themselves.

The man was a radical, a reformist possibly a revolutionary like those that had overthrown the natural order in France. Small wonder that his oldest daughter, was so outspoken and ignored the dictates of society. Then an image of Lucy filled Richard's head, and he forgot his reservations about the man's political leanings and decided instead that Mr Halston was an intelligent man and a good landlord.

He tried to attract the attention of his cousin and indicate that the gentlemen had consumed more than enough port and should now join the ladies, but Abingdon was deep in conversation with two young gentlemen who were unknown to him. He had no option but to take them next door himself.

He rapped on the table and then stood up. It was no matter to him either way if they remained where they were, but he refused to spend another minute in the dining room when he could be getting to know the young lady who had caught his attention. His aunt and mother had already decided the Halston family were the least objectionable, and so he felt free to pursue his interest. The fact that both girls were way beneath the touch of either his cousin or himself no longer mattered. Despite her inadequacies, he would get to know Lucy better.

Abingdon was a decent fellow, but prone to procrastination, and having a strong-minded wife could only be beneficial to him. The older Halston woman would be ideal for him. Possibly, for the first time in many generations, the holder of the family title would not leave his heir and estate in disrepair and debt.

The older ladies had seated themselves in small groups around the drawing room and were fluttering and squawking like colourful birds. All the young ladies were sitting together, apart from the one Richard wished to speak to — she was nowhere to be seen. No doubt she had gone to take care of her sister, which was exactly what he would expect a loving sibling to do.

He stepped aside to allow the gentlemen to surge forward, and soon it was impossible to see, despite his height, if his quarry had returned. His cousin tapped his arm and nodded towards the corridor.

'What is it? Is something wrong?'

'I was talking to the brothers of two of the young ladies, and it would appear that word of my unusual method of finding a wife is now common knowledge. Whoever I choose will be forever labelled as having been sold to me by her father.'

'I hardly think that will matter, Abingdon, as once you are married they will find something else to gossip about. Your wife will be the Countess of Abingdon and therefore above such things. I think that Miss Halston could well be the ideal choice for you.'

'I think I might already have decided who will suit me best. It is her sister. She is perfect in every detail. I hardly think her father will object if I choose her instead of her sibling. Having a countess in the family is all that he's concerned about.'

'She is certainly the most beautiful young lady present, and her family have vague connections to the aristocracy already. However, if I were you, I would not make a hasty decision. The reason for this house party is to get to know all the young ladies before making your selection. Our friends will be arriving tomorrow and the next day — better to wait and see how the candidates are viewed by our peers before making the final choice.' Richard waited to see how his cousin reacted.

'As always, you are correct. I will follow your suggestion in this sensitive matter.'

There was no point in remaining in the drawing room, as the one person who was of interest to him was not present, so Richard retreated to his study

* * *

Freddie had returned to the shared apartment and changed into a riding habit, this being the warmest garment she possessed. She felt perfectly well, although she had no desire to eat, and could not spend the remainder of the evening cooped up inside.

'If my sister comes to enquire, tell her I am perfectly well and have gone to the stables.'

Her maid nodded. 'I shall have hot water waiting for you, miss. What do you wish me to put out for you to change into?'

'I shall remain up here, so require nothing but my nightwear. I shall not be gone long, as it will be full dark soon, and I'll not require you on my return. As long as there is water for my ablutions, that will suffice.' She waited until the girl had gone before carefully closing the bed hangings. It might be better if her sister did not know she had gone out and thought she was safe in her bed asleep.

Even though the house was large, Freddie could still hear the clatter of cutlery and voices coming from the dining room. It might have been sensible to send word to the stables that she required a mount, but she was quite capable of tacking up for herself. She intended to ride the best horse in the stables and needed no one's permission to do that. It was fortunate indeed that they kept country hours here, and there was still half an hour of daylight left.

As expected, the yard was quiet, the grooms, stable boys and coachman having a well-earned break before they settled several dozen horses for the night. The accommodation for the animals was divided into a long barn with two dozen stalls, loose boxes facing into the yard for another dozen or so, and several paddocks at the rear of the buildings into which the workhorses could be turned out.

Freddie walked along, talking softly to each equine head that appeared over the stable door. There was a box at the far end which was either unoccupied, or the horse was of an unsociable nature. She was intrigued as to what sort of equine was in there.

The interior of the stable was dark, but she could make out the shape of a huge stallion. His coat was dark but she could not see if he was a bay or entirely black. The sensible thing would have been to invite him to come to her whilst she remained safely on the other side of the wooden door. However, she was not known for taking the easy option, and pushed the bolt across and stepped inside.

The stallion waited until she had bolted the door again before he moved. There was no time to avoid his charge, and she was pinned into the corner by his weight.

'Don't be silly, my boy. I shall not hurt you. Would you not like to go out for a gallop rather than remaining shut up in here?' It was difficult to speak as the air was being crushed from her chest.

The animal's ears had been flattened against his head, his lips curled back and his huge teeth bared ready to savage her. She made no attempt to touch him and spoke again in the same soft, non-threatening way.

'If you would care to move so I can breathe, I shall fetch your saddle and bridle and we can go out together. I don't expect that you will allow me to put on a side-saddle, so I shall ride astride. How does that sound?'

The pressure eased and the stallion's ears pricked. Then he lowered his head and snuffled into her face. She put her arms around him and stroked his neck. When she gently pressed one hand on his chest, he obliged by moving backwards.

'Good boy. Stay here and I shall be back with your accoutrements in a few minutes.'

She reached backwards over the door and somehow managed to fiddle the bolt open — although he seemed friendly now, she did not dare to turn her back on him just yet. In her eagerness to be outside to close the door, she neglected to push the bolt across.

4

Richard decided he would change out of his evening clothes and back into his daywear and then spend the remainder of the evening outside. It was pitch-dark and freezing, so he put on his greatcoat as well. He would be thought a lunatic for venturing outside unnecessarily in this weather. He had yet to see the quality of the horseflesh brought by these unwelcome visitors — one could usually tell the calibre of a gentleman by his horses.

He was still some distance away from the stable yard when he heard raised voices. Something was obviously amiss, and he increased his pace. As he walked under the arch, he was met by the head groom. The man's face was pale. Something catastrophic had occurred.

'What is it, man? Tell me at once.'

'It's Othello, sir. He's gone. We

cannot find him anywhere and fear he has been stolen.'

Richard swore. 'What do you mean? Was his box door left open? Are you suggesting that someone in my employ was negligent?'

'No, sir; we only realised he had gone a few moments ago. The stable doors were closed and bolted, and I just assumed one of the grooms had already settled him for the night.' He scratched his head. 'It were only because his water hadn't been replenished that we discovered he was gone. I have spoken to everyone and they're adamant they didn't go near the box. He don't tolerate anyone apart from yourself or me dealing with him, and no one wants to be savaged.'

Something occurred to Richard. 'Have you checked if his tack is still there?'

The man's mouth fell open in shock. 'No, I ain't done so. Like I said, Mr Finchley, he wouldn't let no one near enough to put it on.' The fact that it was dark made this line of enquiry seem a tad foolish.

The tack room was in a row of buildings to the rear of the stable yard along with the fodder room, and the barn storing hay and straw. The saddle and bridle were not there. For a moment, Richard could not assimilate this astonishing fact. As far as he was aware, all his guests were in the dining room. Who could possibly have come out here and taken his horse?

Then he understood what had occurred. 'Othello has indeed been stolen. There are Romany in the area; I rode him past their camp the other day. These travelling folk have a way with horses, and even an animal as unsociable as mine might have succumbed to their blandishments.' He thought for a moment before coming to a decision. 'I will take Bruno and go in search of my horse. I shall need two grooms, well-armed, to accompany me.'

As he was the magistrate for this area, he could decide what would be done to the perpetrators of this crime. The punishment for theft of even the smallest item was imprisonment, transportation or even the gallows. If he could recover the horse unharmed, then he would just have the gypsies removed from his land and banned from ever returning to the neighbourhood. He had no wish to see anyone dangle on his behalf.

A short while later, Richard was trotting down the lane thanking the good Lord that it was a full moon, as the lanterns the grooms were carrying barely gave enough illumination to see. He could see the smoke from the caravans half a mile ahead. They had not gone.

He had a good relationship with these strange people, allowed them to camp in the woods and hunt freely for their food. They had never outstayed their welcome, upset any of his tenants or the villagers, so why would they ruin all that by stealing his most valued possession? It didn't make sense.

He pulled his horse to a halt and waited impatiently for the two grooms to arrive at his side. 'I think I might have got this wrong; I've no wish to offend them by false accusations. Remain here and I shall go and speak to their leader.'

When Richard rode into the camp, he was greeted by the usual smiles. There were two roaring fires burning in the clearing, which made it easy to see. The man who ran this band walked across to speak to him.

'Someone has stolen my stallion. I'm hoping that someone here might have seen something and be able to point me in the right direction.'

The man nodded and turned to speak to the others who were gathered behind him. He spoke in their own language for a few moments and then turned back. 'Your horse has not been seen, master. Whoever took him has not ridden this way.'

Richard nodded, relieved he had not accused them of something they had obviously had nothing to do with. He raised his whip in salute and trotted back to join his companions. On the ride back, he was formulating a plan to search the area more methodically in the morning.

★ ★ ★

Freddie emerged from the tack room with the heavy saddle over one arm and the bridle in her other hand. She walked straight into a solid wall of horseflesh.

'Good heavens! What are you doing here, Othello?' She had seen the name written above the tack and knew at once it had to be the black stallion it was referring to.

The horse whickered and slobbered on her shoulder. She guided him easily with her hand on his neck until he was standing parallel to the mounting block. There was no way she could reach him otherwise. As he was so cooperative, they were ready to go in a few minutes.

Her riding habit had a divided skirt, so she could ride astride as easily as she could on a side-saddle without causing a scandal by showing her ankles. Although it was unlikely anyone would see them anyway, as it was now almost dark.

Before she mounted, she tethered him to an iron ring in the wall and quickly closed both doors of the stable. She settled into the saddle and gathered the reins. 'We had better stick to the open paths, my boy, as it will be dark shortly and I don't wish to be in the wood when that happens.'

His ears flicked back and forth as if he was listening to her babbling, and she couldn't stop herself from laughing out loud. They had just left the stable yard when two large grey dogs appeared at her side, obviously intending to accompany her. At least with them beside her, there was no danger of her becoming lost in the darkness.

The ground was firm underfoot, the air crisp and dry, perfect for riding if only it was lighter. She took the path that led around the acres of neatly grazed grass and pushed Othello into a canter. His mouth was light and he responded to the slightest pressure. She had never ridden a horse of his calibre before, and she was loving every moment of it.

The fact that the stallion must belong to the formidable Mr Finchley, that he would be incandescent with rage if he ever discovered she had borrowed his horse without his permission, bothered her not one jot. If he hadn't annoyed her, she would not have eaten the fish that so violently disagreed with her; therefore in some convoluted way, he had only himself to blame for her misbehaviour.

They stayed out far longer than she had intended, as there was sufficient moonlight to see her way. With her canine companions trotting along beside them, she explored the grounds and was determined to have a better look in daylight. It had not occurred to her that anyone would have noticed the horse was missing in her absence. She naturally assumed that they would believe the stallion was still inside his stable and not check for themselves.

A church clock struck seven as she approached the stables. Her heart dropped to her boots. The place was full of noise and raised voices. She could hardly return the horse unnoticed now, and had no notion how to extricate herself from this disaster.

No doubt someone had already discovered she had taken the saddle and bridle, so they would know the horse had not inadvertently wandered off by himself. There was only one thing she could do, and that was hide somewhere until the stable hands retired, and then she could take Othello back.

She kept him on the grass so their passage would be silent and guided him to the rear of the building, ducked low in the saddle, and took him into the hay barn.

'It's warm in here, old fellow, and you will not go hungry. I'll fetch you some water and stay with you until I can put you back in your own box.'

When she dismounted, the two hounds approached her for a fuss, and she was only too happy to oblige. She much preferred the company of dogs and horses to people, and they seemed to sense that. She removed the saddle and bridle, confident the horse would not try and escape even though he was untethered. She crept about the place and successfully discovered a horse blanket and a bucket of freshly drawn water.

Once the stallion was happily munching, she made herself a nest in the loose hay and dropped into it. Immediately the dogs curled up beside her, and she was grateful for their warmth. She must have drifted off to sleep, because when she awoke the place was silent, with only the eerie calls of the owls for company. She was stiff with cold and had difficulty getting back to her feet.

'Come along, Othello. You must go back to your proper place.' Again, all

Freddie had to do was rest her arm on his neck, and he allowed himself to be guided out of the hay barn and around to the stable yard. His stable had been left open, so it was the matter of minutes to take him in, check he had water and that his manger was full. She stroked his velvety nose and he rested it on her shoulder for a second.

'I shall see you tomorrow, that is if I am not evicted from the place.'

Like a burglar, she slipped out and rebolted both doors. She wasn't sure where the dogs slept, but as they remained glued to her side, she assumed they were allowed in the house. Only as she approached the building did it occur to her she might have been locked out.

She tried the door she had exited by and breathed a sigh of relief when it opened beneath her touch. There was a second set of beautifully carved wooden stairs which led directly to the guest wing, and she took those instead of risking being seen. There were occasional wall sconces burning with fresh candles, so she was able to make her way back without difficulty. When she reached her bedchamber, the dogs were still with her, and she was at a loss to know what to do with them.

'You had better come in, but you must be very quiet and not wake my sister.' The only sound they made was the thumping of their tails against the panelling. Even if the hounds were allowed inside the building, she was certain they would not be allowed upstairs, but she would not worry about this now. Tonight they must remain with her, and she would get up at dawn and let them out.

They flopped down at the end of her bed as if this was their usual place to slumber. She removed her garments, had a cursory wash, pulled on her nightgown and scrambled into bed. The chambermaid had built up the fire, so both the dressing room and her room were delightfully warm.

The dogs woke her by pushing their cold muzzles into her face. It was still dark, but they must be eager to go outside and relieve themselves. Not wishing for there to be an unfortunate accident that she would have to explain, Freddie pushed her feet into her slippers, snatched up her thick cloak and swirled it around her shoulders. She paused just long enough to ignite a candle to take with her.

'Come along, boys. I shall let you out.'

They vanished into the early morning darkness and she closed the door behind them. Her stomach rumbled loudly. She could not possibly wait until breakfast was served, but would go and find herself something to eat in the kitchen.

* * *

Richard had gone to bed in a foul humour. Not only had his beloved stallion been taken, but also his dogs. Whoever had done this would live to regret it. He found it difficult to sleep, and just before dawn decided to put on his bedrobe and go into his sitting room to find himself something to read.

He stopped to look around the curtain, wondering if it might have snowed overnight. To his delight, he saw his hounds streak past. Where the devil had they been all night? They must have escaped from whoever kidnapped them and made their way home.

Should he take the time to get dressed, or go and call them as he was? He decided on the latter and, his bare feet making no sound, he raced through the house, his candle aloft, intending to go through the drawing room and open the French doors which led onto the terrace.

He was in the grand hall when he heard footsteps. Immediately he doused his candle and reversed the heavy silver candlestick to use as a weapon. His eyes quickly adjusted to the darkness and he followed the noise.

If he was not mistaken, the burglar was heading for the kitchens. Why the devil would they do that? The silver room was in the opposite direction, as were all the other valuables. He was able to finger his way down the staircase and along the icy passages. Then his blood curdled as there was an unearthly scream, followed by the sound of breaking crockery.

He threw open the door to the main kitchen and rushed in, then collided with something, and his feet went from under him. He landed painfully on his face. For a few moments he was stunned, but was about to push himself upright when a voice he recognised spoke to him from the darkness.

'I am so sorry. I walked into the dresser and tumbled backwards. You tripped over me as you came in.'

'Stay where you are, Miss Halston. I know where to find illumination. I spent many happy hours baking cakes in here when I was small.' He then realised he should have enquired if she was hurt before issuing orders. 'Have you injured yourself? Did I hurt you

72

when I trod on you?'

'I believe I have a nasty gash on my arm which will need attention, but apart from that I am perfectly well, thank you.'

He was on his feet before she had finished speaking. 'Hold something against the cut to stem the bleeding until I can see to it.'

It took him far longer than he wanted to find a taper and push it into the embers in the range. Once he had that alight, he lit as many candles as he could find. He snatched up a handful of clean cloths and turned to the woman still huddled on the floor.

'God's teeth! You should have said how bad it was. Quickly, let me see.' He had never seen so much blood. The woman was covered in it; she was deathly pale and almost comatose.

The blood was coming from her upper arm, and he ripped the sleeve of her sodden nightgown away and then pressed a wad of cloth on the deep gash. She was incapable of assisting him

73

and he needed to find something to use as a bandage.

Then the kitchen door opened and the housekeeper and butler, more or less correctly dressed, burst in, only just managing to avoid treading on the pair of them.

Bevan took charge. 'Mr Foster, send someone to fetch the physician. Mr Finchley, sir, I shall fetch the bandages I keep prepared. I shall not be a moment.'

Richard was becoming increasingly concerned about the condition of the injured woman. Her lips were a worrying blue and her breathing was shallow. Her skin was cold to the touch.

The housekeeper deftly bandaged the pads in place and then stood up. 'She needs to be somewhere warmer, sir. I shall send for — '

'I can manage. Have warming pans and hot bricks sent up to her bedchamber. Bring wine diluted with hot water — I recall when I had a similar injury many years ago that is what was prescribed to replace the blood that had been lost.'

He rocked back onto his feet, slid one hand beneath her knees and the other around her shoulders, and stood up. She was surprisingly light for such a tall woman. The house was coming alive, and footmen were rushing about lighting the sconces, making his journey far easier.

Two maids were dressed and waiting to receive the patient. As Richard put her gently into her bed, her sister burst in.

'Freddie, what has happened to you? Oh dear! I cannot abide the sight of blood. I fear I am going to faint if I remain here.' She retreated, leaving him alone with the maids.

'We shall take care of Miss Halston now, sir.'

His feet were like ice blocks, and from their expressions the servants were shocked that he was in his nightwear. God knew what they were thinking about the fact that their mistress was in a similar state. As he was about to leave, something caught his eye. He looked more closely. He was not mistaken; there were grey dog hairs all over the carpet at the end of the bed.

How his animals had ended up in this woman's bedchamber he had no notion — but he was damned well going to find out as soon as she was well enough to speak to him.

5

Freddie was vaguely aware of her surroundings, and that people were talking, but she could not quite grasp what they were saying or what was happening to her. At some point, a doctor tormented her by putting in sutures, and after that everything went black.

'Freddie, you must wake up and drink this. The doctor was most insistent on this point.'

Groggily, she forced her eyes to open. No sooner had she done so than her sister put a goblet against her mouth and tipped it. There was no alternative but to swallow the contents. This was repeated several times before she became fully awake.

'Thank goodness. You look more the thing now, dearest. You gave us all a dreadful scare.'

'I don't want any more watered wine, Lucy. What I want is something to eat.' She attempted to push herself upright, and a searing pain went through her injured arm. Her sister immediately assisted, and together they got her in a position she was comfortable with.

'I shall send Mary to fetch you something. I assume that you don't wish to have gruel and dry bread.'

'I certainly don't. I want something substantial.'

Her sister didn't bother to ring the bell but went in search of the maid herself. There was something bothering Freddie, but she couldn't quite think what it was. Then the events of the previous evening returned to her in all their dreadful clarity.

She flopped back on the pillows, scarcely able to breathe, as she recalled how Mr Finchley had been obliged to come to her aid for a second time in less than a day. She took several deep, steadying breaths and opened her eyes. She had not been mistaken — the room was filled with beautiful flowers.

Lucy returned to her side. 'Where did all these flowers come from?'

'Mr Finchley came in person first thing this morning to enquire how you were doing, and I believe that it was at his instigation the gardeners prepared these vases for you. Papa sent his best wishes and Mama came in person for a brief visit. As you can imagine, she is overjoyed that you have attracted the attention of the Finchley family.'

Freddie smiled wryly. 'Always a silver lining, dearest. You have not yet asked me how the accident occurred — don't you wish to know?' She had no intention of ever speaking about what had occurred before the accident in the kitchen. When she had finished explaining how she had gone down to find herself something to eat, her sister was smiling too.

'I should have thought of it myself, Freddie, and arranged for a tray to be left out in your sitting room. I came upstairs after dinner, but the curtains were drawn about your bed and I decided to let you sleep.'

'There is no need for you to remain up here with me any longer, Lucy. After I have eaten, I think I will sleep again. I imagine that losing so much blood has made me tired.'

'I've no intention of going downstairs if you are not by my side. I'm happy to sit here and do my embroidery whilst you sleep.'

'Our parents will be most displeased if you're not making a push to be sociable.'

'You are wrong on that count. Mama made it quite clear that being seen to be such a caring sister will only serve to enhance my reputation. I fear I shall have to go down to dinner tonight, but until then I'm staying put.'

The rattle of the tray arriving made Freddie's stomach rumble loudly, and they both laughed. They shared the delicious food, and she was feeling well enough to get up. Indeed, no sooner had the thought entered her head than getting up became a matter of urgency.

Once comfortable again, she tottered back to bed with the able assistance of her sister, and was relieved to be off her feet. She was not as well as she had thought.

'Lucy, can you fetch me something interesting to read? I could not embroider even if I wanted to with my arm injured, but I believe I could balance a book on my lap and turn the pages easily enough.'

'There must be a library somewhere. I shall ask to be directed to it and find you something dull and worthy — exactly the sort of thing you prefer.'

'If there is anything about animal husbandry, art, or politics, that will be ideal. Even a novel, if it is written in French or Italian, would suffice.'

* * *

Richard decided to forego breakfast and set out immediately in search of his stallion. He was about to leave his rooms when his valet rushed in.

'I have just had a message from the stables, sir. Your stallion has been returned and is safe and well in his box.'

He could scarcely believe what he had been told; but then something extraordinary, something even more incredulous, occurred to him. It would explain the dog hairs in Miss Halston's bedchamber. He removed his riding coat and tossed it to his man, which gave him a precious few moments to compose himself before answering.

'That is good news indeed. Send word to the head gardener that I want whatever flowers are available sent up to Miss Halston with my good wishes.'

He had had only an hour or two of shut-eye, as he had not retired until he had been certain she was no longer in any danger. Dr Cunningham was to return later today to check on his patient but had left confident she would make a full recovery.

Richard strolled to his sitting room and stood gazing out of the window across the frost-silvered park. Was it possible this lady had somehow managed to ride his stallion? Othello was infamous for his savagery, and none of the grooms would approach him unless forced to. Yet, if he had got his facts straight, last night Miss Halston had achieved the impossible.

A reluctant smile curved his lips. This woman was an original. She might not be as beautiful as her younger sister, but he had never met anyone, male or female, who was as fearless. He would keep this information to himself for the moment, but when she was recovered he would make sure that she understood exactly how he felt about her actions. He was confident she would not attempt anything of the sort again when he was done with her.

When he enquired, he was told by Lucy that her sister was sleeping and much improved. Satisfied everything was as it should be, he headed for the breakfast room, confident that the majority of the guests would remain in their rooms and have their breakfast sent up on a tray.

His cousin greeted him by waving a laden fork in his direction. 'It would seem that you had an exciting night, Finchley. Get yourself something to eat and tell me all about it.'

Richard was careful not to mention the temporary absence of his dogs and horse, and it would seem that word of this had not spread from the stable yard.

'I suppose I should have got up to see what all the fuss was about, but I had drunk too much claret so remained where I was. I'm glad she is not seriously hurt. How long will she be obliged to remain in her chambers?'

'I've no idea, no doubt the doctor will be able to tell us when he visits this afternoon. I have given instructions to the kitchen that no fish is to be served, and that there will be less of the rich sauces poured over everything.'

Abingdon looked puzzled. 'I thought you enjoyed the elaborate cooking of your French chef. He is certainly the envy of your neighbours.'

'I intend to pass him off to Tewkesbury as soon as I can. In fact, when I have finished here, I'm going to send a message to that effect in the hope that he will be gone from here by tomorrow.'

'Devil take it! You cannot interfere in the running of the house like that, Finchley. You must consult with our parents. It is their job to run the household, not yours.'

Richard swallowed before answering. 'I am master here. If I wish to dismiss the chef, then I shall do so.'

'That's all very well, old fellow, but we have hundreds of people to feed over the festive period, and can hardly do so successfully without him to direct operations.'

'There is a veritable brigade below stairs; he does not do it on his own. I'm certain the cook who ran the kitchen before his arrival has remained in my employ, and she can resume her position.'

This was an extraordinary conversation to be having, as Abingdon was correct that gentlemen did not usually concern themselves with such domestic matters. He returned to his plate, and they ate in companionable silence until the sound of laughter approaching warned him they were about to be joined by some of the young gentlemen who were staying at the house.

'I shall leave you to greet the guests who are arriving today. I shall see you at dinner, no doubt.'

Richard nodded politely at the group as he passed, and was unbothered that they had fallen silent and parted like the Red Sea on his approach.

He was busy with estate business that afternoon when there was a knock on the study door and his mother came in.

'Finchley, what is this I am hearing about you parading around the place in your nightclothes and bare feet?'

'I'm sure that you know the full story, Mama, so there's no necessity for me to explain. You will be pleased to know that Miss Halston will make a full recovery and be able to rejoin the party in a day or two.'

She stared at him through narrowed eyes. 'I don't think you quite understand the predicament you have placed yourself in. I should think the entire household is now aware that you were downstairs with an unmarried lady and both of you in your nightclothes.'

Slowly he put his pen down and stood up so he was towering above her. 'Madam, if you are suggesting that we are compromised and that I now have to offer for her, you have sadly missed the mark. I doubt that Miss Halston was even aware of my presence, as she was already semi-conscious when I arrived.'

Her rigid stance relaxed. 'Well that is a relief, my dear. I have no wish for our families to be associated any more closely than we have to be. Abingdon might be obliged to marry beneath him, but that will not do for you.'

Freddie was told by the doctor that she could get up as soon as she felt well enough. 'Of course, Miss Halston, you will not be able to use your arm for a while. It is fortunate indeed that you are left-handed. You must keep your right arm in your sling at all times, which might make it difficult for you to join the other guests for the next few days.'

'Thank you, sir, I shall follow your instructions. When will you return to remove the stitches?'

'They must stay in for six or seven days — I shall return after Boxing Day to take them out.'

He nodded and left her to her thoughts, and they were not happy ones. If she was incarcerated in her apartment, she would not be able to interfere with the earl's pursuit of her sister in the way that she had planned.

Therefore, she had no alternative but to appear in whatever gown she could wear whilst still having her right arm pinned to her bosom. 'Mary, are all my day dresses with sleeves, or do I have something else I could wear? I cannot wear a spencer, but I think if I have something with short sleeves, I could put a shawl around my shoulders and still be warm enough.'

'I shall look through your closet, miss, and see if there is anything I can alter for you. Are you intending to remain where you are, or do you wish to sit next door?'

'Apart from feeling a little weaker than usual, and my upper arm aching unpleasantly, I am perfectly well. My bedrobe is loose-fitting, and the sash can be tied with my arm inside. I should like you to braid my hair, but there's no necessity to put it up if I'm to remain in my apartment.'

Her maid went in search of suitable garments, leaving Freddie to curl up in a comfortable armchair in front of the fire. With a blanket over her knees, she was more than warm enough. She glanced at the clock and saw it was now approaching the time when her sister would come back to change for dinner.

What news would there be of the new arrivals? All the guests must now be in residence, and she was determined to go down and mingle tomorrow even if she could not dine with them. Neither of her parents had been to see her, and she wasn't sure if she was offended or relieved at this omission.

Lucy hurried in a few minutes later, bursting with news. 'You are the talk of the drawing room, Freddie. Word of your exploits has circulated, and it seems that opinion is divided. Some think that Mr Finchley is a hero stepped in to rescue a maiden in distress, but others are saying this was a midnight tryst that went wrong.'

'Good gracious! That cannot please him one jot. I cannot see why anyone should think we would wish to meet each other in the middle of the night when we were only introduced a few hours ago.'

'Don't forget, dearest, that when you left the dining table last night, he followed after you, and he was gone a considerable time and you did not come back at all.'

'I had forgotten about that. I must write to him at once and put his mind at rest. I've no wish for him to think he has to make me an offer in order to save my good name.'

Her sister was obliged to hold the paper still whilst she penned the letter. She read it through a second time and decided it would do.

Dear Mr Finchley,

Thank you for the beautiful flowers that you sent me. You will be relieved to know that I am making a rapid recovery and will be able to join your guests tomorrow.

I wish to make it clear that I have no wish to marry you, and you must not feel obliged to make me an offer because of the gossip

about the incident last night.
Sincerely yours,

She sanded it, folded it, and her sister applied the required blob of hot wax to seal it shut. 'Get Mary to deliver it to his valet immediately. He should still be in his apartment changing for dinner.'

'I have no time to talk further at the moment, but if you are still awake when I come up this evening, I will speak to you then.' Her sister dashed away to get ready for dinner.

The meal would be fetched up to her after dinner had been served to the guests. She was looking forward to it, as it seemed a long time since she had eaten. A small table had been set out ready to receive the meal, and she wandered across to straighten the silver cutlery and adjust the crystalware.

When there was a tap on the sitting-room door, she thought it to be the tray arriving and called out for the footman to enter. But Mr Finchley stepped in, and he did not look at all pleased to see her. In fact, his expression sent warning shivers up and down her spine.

The fact that she was alone and in nightwear should have been enough for him to retreat — but his only nod to etiquette was to leave the door ajar. Then she saw he was holding her letter in his fingers.

He waved it slowly in front of her. 'Miss Halston, to say that I was astonished to receive this note from you is an understatement. I can assure you that I have no intention of making an offer now or at any time in the future. I do hope that will set your mind at rest on this matter.' The words were innocuous enough, but his tone was decidedly unpleasant. He was looking down his aristocratic nose as if there was a nasty smell in the room and it emanated from her direction.

'Then on that we can agree, sir. You might think yourself a desirable parti, that every unmarried young lady is desperate to become your bride; but I find you arrogant, rude and unpleasant.' She looked pointedly at the door, but he didn't move. His jaw was rigid and she could almost hear his teeth grinding.

6

Richard had not come in here with the intention of doing any more than putting the woman firmly in her place; of letting her know that her impertinence was not appreciated. But being so summarily dismissed by such as she made him speak intemperately.

'Whilst I am here, miss, I shall tell you that you may consider yourself fortunate that you are not now languishing in the county jail. Stealing a horse is a hanging offence, and I am the magistrate and would have no compunction in pressing for the gallows if you have the temerity to take my horse again.' No sooner had he spoken than he wished the words unsaid.

What little colour she had drained away, and she stared at him in shock. He was about to apologise profusely, take back his stupid comment, but she pushed herself upright and took two steps forward so she was no more than an arm's reach from him.

'It is always satisfactory, sir, to have one's opinion confirmed so comprehensively. I shall add to my list of your faults that of being a vicious bully. Now, you will do me the courtesy of removing yourself from my presence.'

He hesitated for a second, but thought it would be wise to do as she said and not compound the offence. For some reason, he was reluctant to turn his back on her, as if he thought she might plunge a knife between his shoulder blades. She had already deeply wounded him with her metaphorical knife. Instead, he backed away and didn't turn until he was safely at the door.

On his return to his apartment, he screwed up the letter and threw it into the fire. What in God's name had possessed him to threaten the poor woman with hanging? He had always thought himself a person who could be relied upon for his common sense and wisdom. Yet, he had just spoken to a defenceless young lady in such terms that would have reduced most to sobs.

He was deeply ashamed of his behaviour. She had called him a vicious bully, and after what he had just done she was justified in that opinion. She might not be from the same social class as himself, but he could not help but admire her fortitude, courage and horsemanship. In fact, he was beginning to think of her more favourably than he did her lovely sister.

His mother was right to say such a liaison would be unsuitable for a gentleman such as himself, so he would do everything in his power to resist the attraction he was beginning to feel. Meanwhile, he must make amends for his brutish behaviour and give the matter some thought before he made a rash move that might be misconstrued. He had no wish to give further fuel to the gossips.

His house was overfull of strangers,

but the addition of his friends and their families did much to improve the situation. At least now he had people of his own class to talk to. He paused at the gallery to stare down into the hall, and even in his curmudgeonly state he could not fail to have his spirits lift at the sight of the festive decorations.

The fat beeswax candles were now burning, and they sent a flickering golden glow onto the glossy green leaves of the evergreen garlands. The holly berries gleamed red amongst the foliage, and the gold and red ribbons just added to the charm.

The yule log had been lit, and the space below him was far warmer than it was usually. He could not fail to notice the kissing bough constructed from mistletoe, ribbons and ivy that hung in prominent position in the centre. Having it attached to the crystal chandelier was perhaps not the best option, but he had to admit he rather liked the effect.

In better humour, Richard strode

downstairs and joined the press of people. He was unsurprised that the room had somehow become divided into two halves — at one end were the candidates and their families, and at the other were the members of the *ton*.

This gave him pause. If the two spheres could not even mingle at a private house party, how could the daughter of one of them hope to fit into his family? He was going to speak to Abingdon and convince him that for all their sakes, he must abandon this ridiculous scheme and accept help from one of his own.

He nodded briefly as he made his way to join his peers, but made no effort to speak to any of them. He was greeted heartily, and soon forgot his disquiet and relaxed in the company of those he was pleased to call his friends.

Although his dining room was commodious, it could not seat so many, so the breakfast room had been laid up to accommodate the overflow. When Foster announced that dinner was served he was unsurprised to see that his friends and family occupied the main room and the others were relegated to the smaller chamber.

★   ★   ★

Freddie paced her sitting room with growing agitation. It might be three days until the Lord's birthday, but she was determined to leave the premises and take her sister with her. She had never liked those of the upper classes, and the behaviour of their host had just confirmed her opinions.

She called out to her maid and Mary came in. 'I wish you and Polly to pack our trunks. We shall be leaving here first thing in the morning.'

The girl opened and shut her mouth but then wisely refrained from comment. 'Yes, miss.'

'We will not speak of this to anyone. Is that quite clear? You and Polly will naturally accompany us.'

She and Lucy would have to depart without their parents, as there was no likelihood of persuading them that this enterprise must be abandoned forthwith. She could not wait to return to her home, to her dogs and horses. Travelling so far without a gentleman might be considered reckless, but she dismissed that idea immediately. She and Lucy would be chaperoning each other, and they had their maids as well. There would be two outriders, plus the coachman and a groom, to keep them safe.

They would have to leave before any of the household was awake, as if word got to her father, he would put a stop to it. It did not get light until seven o'clock, but she thought it would be safe to set out earlier than that if they did not travel fast.

She rang the bell and told her maid to take a message to Sydney, the coachman, to have the carriage outside at six o'clock. It was quite possible the servants would know of their departure long before the Finchleys or her parents did, but if luck was on their side this information would remain a secret until it was too late to prevent their departure.

She devoured the contents of the tray when it arrived, knowing it might be a long time before she ate again. Her ensemble had been set out ready for the morning as well as her cloak, muff and bonnet. The muff would be useless in the circumstances, as she only had one hand to put inside it.

Freddie examined the items and realised she would be unable to wear the gown if she kept her arm tied to her chest. Tomorrow she would get her maid to release her so she could dress normally. The sling could be refashioned once she was dressed. If she didn't do this she would be obliged to travel in her undergarments and cloak.

Her sister could not be expected to return before midnight, which meant somehow she had to find something to occupy her time for another six hours. However, at a little after nine o'clock, Lucy appeared.

'You're fortunate, dearest, that you did not have to endure the embarrassment that I did this evening. The guests were divided into those who were acceptable and those who were not. I'm sure that we were given the same dinner, but it could not have been made plainer. Even our parents were dismayed by the segregation.'

'But what about afterwards? Surely things were different then?'

'One might have thought they would be, but it was worse, if anything, than before. The grand folk remained at one end of the drawing room and the rest of us were at the other. I have never been so humiliated in my life.'

'In which case, Lucy, you will be happy that I have put in motion our immediate departure from here. Our trunks are being packed at this very moment and we shall leave before dawn.'

'I take it you do not have permission for this?'

'Of course I do not. Sit down, and I

will tell you why I am determined not to spend a moment longer here than I must.'

When she had completed her story, her sister was appalled. 'I can hardly credit that a gentleman should speak to you in such a way. The man is a monster, so stuffed full of pride he cannot see how unacceptable his behaviour is. I shall be delighted to leave here and forget that we ever agreed to it.'

'Why don't you sleep in my bed tonight? That way we can be sure we are both awake in good time and you can help me dress.'

* * *

When they crept from the house, Freddie almost lost her footing and was obliged to clutch hold of her sister to stay upright. 'It is lethal underfoot, Lucy, but hard ground will make for easier going as long as the coachman keeps the team to a sensible pace.'

The carriage was waiting, the horses stamping and jangling their bits and impatient to be off. The trunks were safely stowed at the rear and the two outriders standing by their mounts. They were holding lanterns on poles, and the ones on the carriage were also glowing in the darkness.

She scrambled inside, followed by her sister and the two maids. The interior of the carriage was icy and she wished she had been able to arrange for hot bricks for their feet. At least there were the furs to put around their knees.

As soon as they were inside, one of the outriders folded up the steps and closed the door. The carriage rocked and then pulled away. Freddie was too cold and miserable to begin a conversation. Her arm was sore, and she regretted the fact that she had had to disobey the physician's instructions.

Mary and Polly huddled together on the other side of the carriage, and she and her sister did the same. Eventually Freddie dozed off and didn't wake until someone hammered on the window.

'Mary, quickly see what is wrong.' The carriage was stationary, and if it were possible, the interior was even colder.

When her maid let down the window, she recoiled as a drift of icy snow enveloped them. They were apparently stuck in a blizzard in the middle of nowhere.

★   ★   ★

Richard retreated to his study at the earliest possible opportunity after dinner. The atmosphere in the drawing room was poisonous — unless something was done, the house party would be an unmitigated disaster for all concerned.

There was only one thing he could think of that would make any difference. His cousin must declare his ridiculous enterprise cancelled. This would mean that either the unwelcome families would depart in high dudgeon, or they would no longer feel they had to compete with each other to attract Abingdon's attention.

He was about to send a footman to bring his cousin to the study when Abingdon appeared. 'I say, old fellow, it's a bit rich you hiding in here and leaving me to take the brunt of the unpleasantness. The only young lady worth conversing with has gone upstairs to join her sister.' His cousin scowled and flopped into the nearest chair. 'I had just asked the footman to roll back the carpet so there could be some dancing, but now that seems a waste of time.'

The mention of Miss Halston made Richard feel ashamed all over again. He had still not come up with a suitable scheme to show he was genuinely apologetic for his comments.

'Your decision to have this extraordinary house party is proving to be a dismal failure, my friend. I have no option but to cancel it and for you to allow me to settle your debts, repair your house and put your estates in order. It would not be the first time the Finchleys have come to the rescue of the Abingdons.'

'I am reluctant to admit that you are right, and I shall accept your generous offer. Tomorrow I shall tell everyone that I'm no longer intending to marry the highest bidder. It's hardly a festive atmosphere out there, and I fear such an announcement will make matters worse.'

'They could not be any worse. However, I do not think it wise to speak of your decision so publicly. Let our parents take care of that. I shall send for my lawyers to visit in the new year and will get matters settled then.'

'There are still three days left before Christmas Day. Do you think that will be time enough to improve the situation?'

'I have a deal of fence-mending to do with Miss Halston. I was unpardonably rude to her, and I cannot think of a way to make amends. Have you any suggestions?'

'As she cannot come down because of her injury, I can't think that you can do anything about it at the moment. I think we must organise a treasure hunt and offer a substantial prize of some sort to the winning team.'

Richard frowned. 'I cannot see how that will help improve the situation. Not only are half the guests not speaking to the other half, but even amongst those who are already friends there is backbiting and unpleasantness.'

'I think I am more aware of that than you, cousin, as you have kept yourself apart from the fray. I shall put all the names of all the participants in a hat, and then they shall be drawn out one by one so that the teams will be randomly assembled.' He chuckled at Richard's incredulous expression. 'I know it sounds ridiculous, but only the younger members will wish to participate, and I doubt that they will be as bothered as the older ones about who they are paired with.'

'I believe that it might work. If you

would care to go and speak to my mother, I shall start assembling the clues. I think we must hold this treasure hunt the day after tomorrow — hopefully, by then our guests will be eagerly anticipating the hunt. I might make it a combination of puzzles and searching for particular items.'

'I have not seen you so enthused for a long time, Finchley. I shall leave you to it and go and speak to Mama. Do you wish me to come back and assist you?'

'No, but if one of your sisters could come and act as my scribe, I should be grateful.'

With the help of his cousin Amanda, the oldest, Richard now had all the names of the unmarried guests written neatly on strips of paper. These would be folded up and put into a hat to be drawn out later.

'Thank you, Amanda. Your help was invaluable. I can hear the sound of the piano being played, so they must be dancing. Go and join them — I do know how you love to dance.'

'Thank you, Cousin Richard. If you are quite sure you do not need me anymore, I shall return to the drawing room. I cannot wait to tell everyone about your plans for this treasure hunt — I believe they will be as excited as I am at the prospect. I cannot remember the last time anything half as exciting took place here.'

Richard smiled. He had deliberately asked for one of his female cousins to join him on the pretext of writing out the names so that they could go back and spread the word about the forthcoming event. When he had explained to her how the teams were going to be assembled, she had clapped her hands and said that would make it even more exciting.

If the young mixed in together, then their parents would be obliged to do the same. When he retired, the house was quiet, but he had completed the clues and was satisfied they would keep the company entertained.

Despite being tired, he slept fitfully.

111

His guilty conscience would not let him rest. Eventually he gave up trying to sleep and got out of bed. He would not make the mistake a second time of wandering about the house in his nightwear. It took him a while to find the garments he required, but he managed it eventually. Once dressed, he went into his sitting room and trimmed a quill. He sat down at the small desk and tried to compose the most difficult letter of his life.

After half a dozen attempts, all tossed into the fire, he decided he had no option but to speak to her in person. He glanced at the overmantel clock. He thought it likely Miss Halston would be awake by now. She had not been up until the small hours dancing as the others had, and seven o'clock was not so very early after all.

His valet was now banging about preparing his shaving water. He didn't bother to ring the bell, but raised his voice to attract attention. 'Anderson, I wish to know if Miss Halston is awake.

Will you go and enquire?'

Scarcely ten minutes had passed when the man returned. 'Sir, the apartment is empty. Miss Halston and her sister have gone.'

7

Freddie wiped the snow from her face, unsuccessfully attempted to pull up the hood of her cloak over her bonnet, and leaned forward so she could hear what the outrider was trying to say. Most of his words were being blown away by the blizzard.

'The way is blocked, miss. We can't go no further. We're harnessing the team and reckon you can ride to safety.'

'Very well. I shall close the window and we shall remain here until you are ready for us.' She turned to her companions. 'You must leave everything here; the horses will be carrying a double burden already.'

'I have never been on a horse, miss, and I don't know how to ride,' Mary wailed.

'You will be travelling pillion; all you have to do is hold on.' This brisk statement seemed to reassure both of the maids. The interior of the carriage was so dark that Freddie couldn't see her sister, but knew she must be as worried as she was at the outcome of this venture.

'Remove your bonnet, put up your hood and tie your muffler around the outside so it covers the lower part of your face. A muff will be useless, but as we all have warm gloves, we should not suffer unduly from the cold.'

The carriage rocked as all three of her companions did as she suggested. Lucy shuffled up and did the same for her, as any sort of movement with her injured arm was all but impossible. She wasn't sure which of them would be riding bareback on the carriage horses. It would be preferable to be travelling pillion behind one of the outriders, but as she and Lucy were experienced horsewomen, she thought it might be sensible for them to take the least favourable option.

The carriage door opened, and for a

second time they were surrounded by snow. Keeping her head down, Freddie stumbled down the steps, grateful for the assistance of the coachman.

'Can you manage to ride astride, miss? I thought your girls would do better riding pillion.'

'I agree.' She was obliged to shout to make herself heard above the roaring wind. She could scarcely see an arm's length in front of her through the swirling whiteness.

She was tossed astride one of the team, and grabbed a handful of the wiry mane in order to stay in position. As there were no reins, she and Lucy would have to rely on their mounts' common sense. Horses were instinctively herd animals and should wish to stay together.

The lanterns were blowing wildly back and forth, but at least they gave a welcome smudge of light in the whiteness. The six horses travelled nose to tail, and Freddie and Lucy were positioned in the centre of the column.

Heaven knew how far they might have to go before they found shelter from the elements. Freddie doubted any of them would survive for more than an hour or two out here. Even with her head lowered, the snow crept inside, and her extremities were frozen.

They plodded onwards for what seemed an interminable time, but then the horse Freddie was riding increased its pace and they were cantering. If she and her sister hadn't been excellent riders, they would have lost their seats and tumbled to the ground.

There could be only one explanation for this: the lead animal had sensed there was a warm stable ahead and was heading towards it regardless of the dangers that speed might bring to the precariously balanced riders.

Then through the blizzard Freddie saw lights, and all six of them clattered into the yard of a substantial inn. Ostlers appeared, despite the weather and the early hour, and she was assisted to the ground. Her sister and the two maids were also safe, and the horses did not seem to have suffered unduly from the experience.

'Quickly — inside. The landlord is holding the door for us. Sydney, make sure that you and the others find yourselves a comfortable billet after you have taken care of our horses.'

The snow was already ankle-deep, and Freddie trudged through it praying no one else was stranded as they themselves had been.

'Welcome, madam. You are fortunate indeed to have reached my hostelry safely. Were you forced to abandon your carriage on the road? I take it the gentlemen of your party have remained to take care of this matter?'

'Do you have chambers available? We are frozen to the marrow and have no luggage with us — we had to abandon that with our carriage.'

'The girl will take you to what we have available. I fear it's not as commodious as you might have wished, but in the circumstances, I'm sure you'll find it acceptable.'

Freddie followed the diminutive maid, too cold and miserable to worry about anything except getting warm and dry and having a hot drink of some sort.

'There will be hot water sent up directly, madam, and the kitchen is just open. What would you like to break your fast?' The child — she could be little more than ten years of age — curtsied and waited expectantly for her reply.

'Whatever you have will be perfect. Chocolate and coffee if possible but anything hot will suffice.'

The chamber was large enough to contain two beds, a small table with three bentwood chairs around it, and three padded armchairs grouped in front of the roaring fire, but there was no separate sitting room or dressing room.

'Mary, Polly, you will take the bed by the window, and Miss Lucy and I will take this one.'

Freddie stripped off her cloak with difficulty, as her injury was throbbing painfully. She was relieved to see that only the extremities of their garments were wet.

'If we stand in front of the fire and flap our gowns around, I'm sure we will soon dry out.'

They were doing so when two equally small boys staggered in carrying laden trays, followed by the maid with a large jug of hot water. After washing the worst of the journey from their persons, they sat down and ate together; there was no time for etiquette today. It would not be fair to keep Mary and Polly waiting for their meal until the food was unpalatably cold.

★　★　★

Richard did not hesitate. 'Pack my saddlebag, I shall go after them. Send word to the stable that I shall require my horse to be ready for me.'

His cousin occupied an apartment

opposite his own, and he did not knock or wait to be invited in but threw open the bedchamber door. 'Abingdon, the Halston girls have fled. Are you coming with me to find them?'

'I am, of course. I'll meet you in the stables in twenty minutes.'

It was scarcely light, and if Richard were not mistaken, there was snow in the air. He and Abingdon would travel more quickly on horseback than they could possibly do in a carriage, and hopefully they would overtake the party before they got too far.

Initially they travelled across country, but then the weather worsened and it became too dangerous to continue across the landscape, as they could not see properly. Othello was well protected beneath the skirts of his caped riding coat, as was the mount that Richard's cousin was riding.

It took a while to find the road, and by that time Richard realised he could not continue his search, as they would likely lose their lives if they remained out in the elements for much longer.

'Give the horses their heads,' he yelled into Abingdon's ear. 'If there is shelter nearby, they will find it for us.'

When the stallion increased his pace, Richard knew that today would not be the day he met his maker. The horses charged into the yard of a building he assumed was an inn — it was impossible to see more than a yard in front of his face, as the blizzard had worsened. His cousin looked more like a snowman than a human being, and he himself was in little better case. He dismounted and pulled the reins over Othello's ears. 'Come on, old boy. I shall find you somewhere warm and dry. You have done well this morning.'

He was unsurprised that no ostlers had come out to greet them. Nobody with a grain of sense would be abroad in this foul weather. The horses were stabled in a long barn, and as soon as he entered he recognised some of the occupants of the stalls.

'They are here before us. I didn't see

the carriage, so I think they must have abandoned it. There are empty stalls at the far end we can use.'

He had removed the saddle and was about to do the same for the bridle when a stable hand appeared at his side. 'Begging your pardon, my lord. We didn't hear you come in. Leave this fine fellow to me.'

Richard was about to warn the man he might be savaged, but the stallion was too cold and tired to object to a stranger taking care of him.

'Good man. I shall leave them to you. When did those horses arrive here?'

'An hour ago, my lord. The master reckoned gentlemen would be along soon. He has a chamber prepared for you.'

Richard made no reply to this strange remark, but patted his horse and strode down the long building to join his cousin, his saddlebag over his shoulder.

'It seems that we are expected. I hardly think that Miss Halston would have told the landlord we were coming, but it would seem churlish to say anything untoward.'

'We are all lucky to have arrived here unscathed, Finchley. You do realise we will be unable to leave here until the blizzard stops. God knows what will be said about the sudden disappearance of all four of us.'

'As there is nothing we can do about it, my friend, you must thank the Lord we are all alive to face the consequences when we eventually return.' When they stepped back into the blizzard, it seemed to have lessened somewhat. Instead of being crisp underfoot, the snow was slushy. With luck, they would only be gone for the day and would be able to return before there was too much gossip and speculation.

The interior of the inn was as well-maintained as the stables. They were greeted by a jovial landlord. 'I have been expecting you, sirs. When the ladies of your party arrived unescorted, I realised you must have remained behind to ensure the carriage was secure. If you would care to follow that boy, he will take you to your chamber. I apologise that you will have to share, but we are full to bursting because no one can depart owing to the inclement weather.'

'Send something to eat, coffee and hot water to our room. There's no need to disturb the ladies; we will speak to them ourselves when we are refreshed and have removed the grime of the journey from our persons.'

The accommodation was adequate, the room sparkling, the furniture polished; but Richard was not happy about being obliged to share the large bedroom with his cousin. With any luck, they would not have to overnight here and would be able to leave later that day, so the sleeping arrangements would be irrelevant.

After devouring a surprisingly tasty breakfast and drinking two pots of coffee between them, Richard was ready to go in search of the missing ladies.

'Have you thought what you are going to say to explain your unexpected arrival here?'

'I have, but I'm still at a loss to know how best to approach the young lady I so mortally offended. From what we've learned, they are sharing one chamber between four of them. I've no wish to speak to Miss Halston in front of her servants or her sister.'

'In which case, Finchley, why don't you speak to her in here? I'm going in search of the snug to see if I can discover how soon the locals think the road will be clear and the carriage can be collected.'

How could he entice Miss Halston to visit him here? Presumably she was unaware that he had arrived, which might work in his favour. He could write to her, but she might well recognise his handwriting, as it was quite possible she had seen it some-where. No, he would get one of the servants from the inn to deliver a message.

* * *

Lucy and the two maids retired to the beds, but Freddie was in too much pain to lie down. She had made a grave error of judgement running away so precipitously and was now suffering the consequences.

She paced the carpet, nursing her injured arm, and wished she was anywhere but here. The thought of continuing the journey at some point and being tossed about in a carriage for several hours filled her with dread.

There was a knock on the door, and she went to open it herself, not wishing to disturb either Mary or Polly, who were now sound asleep.

'Excuse me, miss, but I'm to tell you there's a chamber become vacant down the hall, and the master wants to know if you would like to have it for yourself and your maid.'

'I certainly would. It is rather cramped in here. Is the room ready for occupation now?'

'It will be very shortly, miss, but perhaps you had better see it before you make your decision. It ain't as big as this one.'

She was led along the passageway and down another. The girl pointed to the open door, but instead of opening it for her, she scuttled off.

The room was similar to the one she had already been allocated. She stepped inside and the door closed behind her. She spun round and was too shocked to do more than stare open-mouthed at the one person she least wished to see.

'Miss Halston. Forgive me for my subterfuge, but I have to speak to you in private. If you give me your word you will not run away, I shall open the door again. I'm sure you do not wish to be closeted in here unchaperoned and with the door shut.'

She tottered to the nearest chair and collapsed on it, unable to make a coherent response. She closed her eyes for a moment, trying to gather her scattered wits.

'How are you here?' This was the best she could come up with.

'When I heard that you had left so suddenly, I had no option but to follow you and try and persuade you to return.'

Wearily she opened her eyes, to find him sitting far too close. If she didn't know him better, she would think that he was genuinely concerned for her welfare. 'You know my opinion of your character, Mr Finchley, so must understand why I cannot remain under your roof. Neither my sister nor myself wish to be associated with your family in any way whatsoever.'

'I understand exactly, my dear. But you must understand I cannot allow you to return to your home when your parents are still residing with me. Your house will be shut down, and there will be no warmth or food available. That would be a wretched way to spend the festive season.'

'What would be even worse, as far as I'm concerned, would be to remain.

The whole escapade was doomed to disaster. I cannot comprehend how my father became embroiled in it.'

'I told my cousin so, and he has now accepted my advice. My guests will already be aware that the earl has changed his mind and will not be selling himself to the highest bidder in exchange for his title.' His smile was warm, and for the first time it was genuine. 'I owe you the most humble and grovelling of apologies. I have no excuse to offer for my discourteous behaviour, but I give you my word as a gentleman that if you return, you will be treated as my most honoured guest.'

Despite her pain, she smiled at his remark. 'I accept your apology, as I believe it to be heartfelt. However, if I do agree to come back, I have no wish to be singled out in any way at all. I believe that I have pointed out to you, on more than one occasion, that I do not want to be thought a candidate for your hand.'

She waited to see if this time she got

another vitriolic comment — after all, when she had said something similar last time, he had threatened to have her sent to the gibbet.

His reaction was totally unexpected. He leaned forward and placed his lips on hers. No more than a gentle pressure, but it sent her pulse skittering.

'You should not have done that. Only a betrothed couple can exchange such intimacies.'

His eyes were dark, his smile wicked. 'Exactly so, sweetheart. I have decided that, despite your obvious drawbacks, I wish to marry you.'

8

'Then you are going to be disappointed, sir, as when I do accept an offer, it will be from a gentleman who not only loves me but also respects my ancestry. You fail on both counts. Remove yourself from this chamber forthwith. I shall pretend that this appalling breach of etiquette never took place.'

This was not the reaction Richard was expecting. He considered himself to be an eligible *parti* — he had an impeccable pedigree, was in his prime, and was one of the warmest men in the county.

Then he understood. He had gone about this in quite the wrong way. He should have spoken to her father first and then made her a formal offer.

'I apologise. I shall go, but I wish to tell you that the weather is improving and we should be able to leave here in an hour or two. With luck, we should be back before anyone has noticed we were gone.' He nodded and smiled, which she did not return, and strolled out confident he would achieve his objective when he approached it in the correct way.

As he was closing the door, he heard her laughing, and for a moment was puzzled. Then the door opened and she stepped out.

'I do beg your pardon, Mr Finchley, from ejecting you from your own room. Whatever the weather is doing, unless the road is cleared, my carriage will remain stuck behind a snowdrift.' She stepped around him, nodded, and vanished around the corner.

He went in search of his cousin and found him sitting comfortably in the snug conversing with others who had been snowbound.

'Welcome, Finchley. These fine fellows have told me they expect to be on their way within the hour. I have sent

Miss Halston's men out to rescue the carriage, and hopefully will be able to dig it out and bring it here so we can all go home.'

Somehow Richard managed to keep his smile in place. He was very fond of Abingdon, but he was the most indiscreet fellow that he knew. He had carefully avoided using names, but now all their identities were revealed, and whatever Frederica's feelings on the matter, she might well find herself betrothed to him whether she wanted it or not.

'If you have finished your ale, there are things we need to discuss.'

Immediately his cousin put down his pot, bid farewell to his temporary friends, and hurried over to join him. 'I know why you are looking at me so fiercely. I should not have mentioned who we are. Does that mean our reputations are in tatters?'

'I have already asked Frederica to marry me — she has refused, but I am sure I will convince her otherwise over the next few days. However, I think you must do the same for her sister.'

'Yesterday you were telling me I must abandon my plans to marry out of my social class, and yet now you are telling me the opposite. You are as variable as a windmill, Finchley, which is not at all like you.'

'I suggest that you go and speak to the lady immediately. We can talk to Mr Halston on our return and make the announcement after dinner.'

'Exactly what announcement would that be, sir?'

Richard was so startled by this sudden appearance of Frederica that he stumbled forward, colliding with his cousin, and together they spun around the vestibule as if engaged in a waltz. By the time they had recovered their balance, the servants were sniggering at their antics, and Frederica was openly laughing.

Richard was not accustomed to being a figure of fun and intended to put her straight on this matter. Then he reconsidered — he could not continue to give her a bear-garden jaw whenever she annoyed him. He would never persuade her to change her mind that way.

'Miss Halston, were you never told that eavesdropping is considered bad manners?'

'This is a public place, Finchley, so anybody in the vicinity could have overheard you. If you do not wish to be humiliated in front of your friends and family, then I suggest that you listen to what I have told you. Neither my sister nor I have any wish to be married to either of you. I don't know how much clearer I can make this.'

Abingdon disappeared up the stairs, not wishing to be involved in this confrontation. Richard moved closer so he and Frederica could speak more privately. 'Whatever your feelings on the matter, my dear, we have been seen in public together, and my cousin identified us all. There is no need for me to elaborate, as I'm sure you understand what this means.'

'What it means, sir, is that my sister

and I will return to our own stratum of society unscathed by the gossip. However, I think that you and the earl will be the subject of malicious tittle-tattle for some time to come.'

He was about to respond with a pithy reply when her sister flew down the stairs and skidded to a halt beside them. 'The earl insists that I must marry him, but I have told him no. I think that our parents are going to be most displeased with us.'

Frederica — Richard refused to think of her as Freddie, as it was an unsuitable name for a young lady in his opinion — nodded; and the only way to describe her expression was gleeful.

'We have achieved our aims most wonderfully, and now we can return and spend Christmas on our own.' Frederica glanced at him to make sure he was listening before continuing. 'Mr Finchley seems to think we will spend a miserable time, as our servants will be unprepared for our arrival. I believe that his staff must be inadequate if that is what he thinks. Our staff, as you know, will have the larders well-stocked and everywhere warm and welcoming before we arrive.'

This was not going according to plan, and Richard was unused to having his ideas thwarted. He could think of only one thing that could prevent the ladies from leaving the house party. It would be underhanded, but he had no choice. Christmas would not be worth celebrating if Frederica was not there to share it with him.

* * *

Freddie put her arm through her sister's and drew her to one side. 'The snow is melting. I'm going to go and find our men and get them to fetch the carriage so we can continue on our journey.'

'We cannot remain down here, as we are attracting too much attention. Shall we return to our chamber until we can leave?'

They did so, and Mary found Freddie some laudanum to ease the pain in her arm. She did not like to take this opiate, but feared she would not be able to complete the journey without it. She checked and found no bleeding, so her sutures had remained in place.

When she told Lucy of Mr. Finchley's uncomplimentary proposal, she had been suitably shocked. 'That man has a very high opinion of himself. How dare he say that he is somehow lowering his standards by offering for you?'

'That was exactly my opinion, dearest, and I think that he will not make the same mistake again. Our parents will indeed be gravely shocked by our immodest behaviour, but better they are upset now than we are unhappy for the rest of our lives.'

★   ★   ★

Two hours passed pleasantly enough, and then word was sent from the stables that the carriage was back and the roads sufficiently clear to depart. They had seen no more of the gentlemen, and for that, Freddie was profoundly grateful.

The snow had melted as quickly as it had come, and the only sign of the blizzard was the grey heaps that had been shovelled from the cobbles and piled against the walls. This time the interior of the carriage was much warmer, and there were hot bricks to rest their feet on. Even the rugs had been somehow dried and warmed.

'I should think that our garments will be in a sad state on our return, having been left out in the elements for so long,' Freddie said. 'It is fortunate indeed that we will not need to be seen in public until well into the new year.'

'Do you think that our mama and papa will remain at Finchley Hall when they discover we have abandoned them?' Lucy asked. As always, they talked freely in front of their maids, as they knew the girls would never reveal anything they heard.

'You are forgetting, dearest, that they cannot leave even if they wished to, as we have the carriage. In all conscience, I cannot send it back until after Boxing Day.'

'Then let us hope, Freddie, that they have forgiven us by the time they do come back. I can imagine how this news will be viewed by all the guests.'

'That is something we no longer have to worry about, Lucy. I have never aspired to join the *ton*. I am perfectly content where I am.'

It had been an arduous few hours, and Freddie drifted off to sleep knowing they were safely on their way and she would never have to speak to Mr Finchley again. He was so high in the instep that she was surprised he could walk at all.

The curtains had been pulled down, so she was unable to see the countryside on either side of the road; but it helped to keep the warmth in, and for that she was grateful. When the carriage rocked to a standstill two hours later, it was too dark to see.

'We have arrived at our overnight stop. Mary, you and Polly must bring in our small boxes, as I wish to be able to change my ensemble before setting out tomorrow.'

The steps were let down and the door opened. 'Allow me to assist you, my dear. I have no wish for you to cause yourself further injury.'

How could this be? Freddie was speechless, which did not happen very often. Her sister was not so afflicted and made her opinions very clear.

'You are despicable, Mr Finchley. You know that we had no wish to return to your house, and yet here we are. The only way this could have been accomplished was if you bribed our servants. I do not know which of these I despise more, you or our disloyal staff.'

The wretched man seemed unconcerned about this tirade. He merely nodded and stepped to one side so they could walk past. The sound of the house party enjoying dinner echoed along the broad passageways. As far as Freddie could see, their arrival was unobserved.

She didn't recover her composure until they were back in the apartment they had abandoned at dawn. 'Did you notice if Finchley and the earl were in evening dress?'

Lucy looked somewhat surprised by this remark, but nodded. 'They were — they must have arrived some time before us. I suppose we must be relieved no one will have guessed they were with us.'

'I see there are trays waiting on the table. I am hungry after all this travelling, but my arm is so stiff and sore I doubt I could cut up my food.'

'Then I shall do it for you, dearest. Let me help you remove your outer garments and boots. Mary and Polly will be busy unpacking the trunks and repairing the damage to our gowns.'

The repast was exactly what they wanted. No sign of rich cream sauces disguising the food; everything was

beautifully cooked with no fish anywhere in sight.

'I am going to retire, Lucy. Would
you be so kind as to help me?' Freddie
was too dispirited to say more.

'I shall remain in here for an hour or
two more, as I'm not yet tired.'

As Freddie was getting comfortable
in bed, she heard voices in the sitting
room and remained still, not expecting
to be disturbed. Then Lucy burst in
looking positively happy.

'One of the young ladies I had become
friendly with has just called in to enquire
if we are both fully recovered. No one
knows of our escapade apart from ourselves and the gentlemen involved.'

'I suppose that's one thing to be
thankful for.'

'Indeed it is, but that is not why I am
looking so much more sanguine. There
is to be a treasure hunt tomorrow, and
the names of the participants were put
in a hat and drawn out. Nobody will
know with whom they are teamed until
tomorrow morning.'

'Both sides of the divide have been mixed together? I hope I am well enough to participate myself, for as you know, I do love a challenge of any sort.'

'I'm sure you will be much better, dearest. Although your arm is painful, you are managing perfectly well without it in that confining sling.'

Freddie flexed her right arm and nodded. 'It is so much better, I think, that I might dispense with the sling altogether tomorrow. Two hours ago I thought it worse, and now I can scarcely feel it.'

Her sister ran across and embraced her. 'I am almost glad that we were fetched back. I have not forgiven them for tricking us, but possibly they were right to do so.'

★   ★   ★

Richard hoped Frederica would be more receptive to his approach when she had had a good night's rest. Her complexion, what he had been able to

145

see of it beneath her bonnet and hood, was pale. She really shouldn't have been gallivanting all over the county whilst her arm was still so fragile.

He and Abingdon had just got back in time to change and appear for dinner. The drawing room had been abuzz with talk of the forthcoming treasure hunt. His ploy to mix the two sides of the party had worked; none of the participants had objected to being teamed with those they were not usually associated with.

Mr and Mrs Halston had remained in ignorance of their daughters' bid for freedom. Maybe luck would hold, and the gentlemen who had seen them at the inn would not bother to talk about it to their wives. Once a woman got hold of a tasty morsel of news, it would spread like wildfire around the county.

Richard used the excuse of needing to complete the clues for tomorrow's much anticipated event in order to escape immediately after dinner. Some-one had been persuaded to play, and

there was to be dancing again tonight.
If only the older members of the party
would agree to interact, then possibly
his ill-thought-out Christmas event
might not be as dismal as he had
feared.

There were to be seven teams of four,
though neither he nor Frederica had
been included for obvious reasons. She
would not be well enough, and he knew
all the answers. This meant there had to
be seven copies of each clue. He could
hardly ask anyone participating to copy
them out, so he must do this irksome
task himself, and it was likely to keep
him up until midnight.

In fact, it was nearer one o'clock in
the morning before the final one was
done. He had arranged with the butler
that three footmen would be given the
task of hiding the pieces of paper first
thing in the morning, before the guests
were up.

He threw a few logs onto the fire and
kicked them with his boot to encourage
the flames to catch. The house was

quiet, but the wall sconces were always left to burn out of their own accord, so it would be a simple matter to return to his apartment without the necessity of taking a candle.

He carefully hid the clues and then poured himself a generous measure of brandy, then moved an armchair in front of the fire, collapsed into it and stretched out his feet. This new fashion of trousers and evening slippers was a great improvement on silk stockings and knee breeches, but he much preferred to be wearing his Hessians.

There was a noise outside the door. Who could be creeping about the house at this time of night? Someone must have come in search of the clues so they could begin solving them and thus win the hunt tomorrow. But they were securely locked in his desk, so there was no danger of that happening. However, Richard was curious to know who the cheat might be. He waited, but the footsteps passed; they had not been coming to his study after all.

He put down his glass and went to investigate. The library was the next chamber, and he could see a flickering light coming from the open door. This was a strange time to be searching for a book, but it behoved him to offer his assistance.

He pushed open the door and came face to face with Frederica. 'I should have known it would be you, sweetheart. You have a propensity for skulking about the place in the dead of night.'

'I found I could not sleep, so have come in search of something to read.' She laughed, and the sound echoed amongst the books. 'I am stating the obvious, as what else would I be doing in your library?'

'Let me help you find something suitable. My mother is overly fond of romantic nonsense. Would you like something of that sort?'

'Normally I would refuse, but tonight I think that is exactly what I would like. Although to be honest, I would exchange any book for a pot of coffee and a slice of plum cake.'

It was Richard's turn to laugh. 'The last time we encountered each other in the kitchen is best forgotten, my dear. We shall find your book, and then you must wait in the study in the warm whilst I go in search of refreshments.'

9

Finchley stepped around her and walked briskly to a polished hexagonal table at the far end of the room. He collected three volumes and returned with them. 'Here you are. I'm sure one of these will suit the purpose exactly.' He smiled, and Freddie could not help but notice he was actually quite an attractive gentleman when he was not being unpleasant.

'I thank you, sir. It is fortunate that we are both correctly dressed. It took me a considerable time to ensure I was decent . . . ' She stammered to a halt and a wave of heat engulfed her. How could she have been so indelicate as to mention something so intimate as removing and replacing her garments?

'Exactly so, my dear. Now, I shall carry your books, and you will accompany me to my study. I believe we are so far beyond the pale that it could hardly matter what we do to upset the tabbies.'

She was ushered into his inner sanctum and looked around with interest. It was much the same as her father's study: bookshelves of leather-bound volumes, a handsome desk, and a collection of both upright and more comfortable seats.

Richard gestured towards the desk and then removed a key from his pocket. 'I would be grateful if you would read through the clues for tomorrow's treasure hunt. It is possible, although unlikely, that you might find room for improvement.' He quirked an eyebrow and she returned his smile.

'I did not know that I had been excluded from this excitement, but I suppose it was wise in the circum-stances. I shall be delighted to pass judgement on your clues.'

He left her to find her own way to his desk and unlock the drawer. There were in fact ten piles neatly tied together with ribbon; she looked through until she found one that was obviously the master copy that included all fourteen clues.

As she flicked through, she saw that not all were puzzles or riddles, but an item that had to be found. The first was a black feather, the second a spherical object, the third a lady's garter. Good heavens! This was a trifle risqué, as she could see it might well involve the removal of such an item from one of the participants. Other bits of clothing needed were a gentleman's neckcloth, a riding glove, and a blue waistcoat.

She had finished reading without feeling the necessity to change a thing when he strode in carrying the tray.

'I have everything we need on here. I added cream and sugar, as I don't know how you prefer to drink your coffee. There is, as requested, a generous slice of plum cake, but also a miscellany of other items I found in the pantry. I hope Cook doesn't think one of the staff has been pilfering.'

'She might well, but that is easily solved if you speak to your valet. Word will soon filter down to the kitchens.' She pointed to the stack of paper. 'I have read all of them and am suitably impressed. I had no notion you were . . . you were so versatile.'

'Did you solve all the riddles?' As he spoke, he was pouring coffee into delicate porcelain cups and placing a selection of items on a matching plate. 'I was not sure about including some of the items of clothing, but thought it added a certain piquancy to the proceedings.'

'It will certainly add something, Mr Finchley. Some of the young ladies will do the correct thing and return to their rooms, but my sister will be one of those who does not. I can see that the most daring of the teams will be the winner of this hunt.'

Richard helped himself and then moved two small tables upon which they could place their cups and plates. They munched and drank without either feeling the need to intersperse eating with trivial conversation.

This was the first time since Freddie had met him that they had managed to be in each other's company for more than five minutes without being at daggers drawn. Replete, she put down her cup and plate and sighed with satisfaction.

'Thank you; that was exactly what I wanted. Have you decided what the prize will be for the winning team?'

He grinned, and it made him look years younger. 'I haven't the faintest notion — I was rather hoping you might come up with a suitable suggestion.'

'Why not make them kings and queens of the company for the day?'

'Exactly what would this entail? I could not countenance anything that might involve making other guests humiliate themselves in any way.'

'I was not thinking along those lines, Mr Finchley. I — '

He interrupted her with a wave of his

hand. 'I am heartily sick and tired of hearing you address me so formally. I wish you to use my given name, and I shall call you Frederica.'

'I might consider it, if I knew what your given name was.'

'Richard. Nobody calls me that, but I believe I should like to hear my name spoken by you.'

'Only my mother calls me Frederica. I am Freddie to my friends.'

'Then you shall be Freddie to me also, as I hope you will count me as your friend one day.'

'To return to the question of the prize. The winners could decide who sits where at dinner on Christmas Eve, also what entertainment is provided, and perhaps open the ball on New Year's Eve?'

'That is acceptable. I shall add something tangible as well; there must be things in the attic that would make good gifts. You must help me find them.'

She yawned loudly. 'I must go back

to my room, or I shall be fit for nothing tomorrow. I give you permission to call me Freddie in private, but you will continue to address me formally in company. The same rules apply to me and the use of your given name.' She avoided giving him an answer to his question about going into the attics.

He rose smoothly to his feet and offered his hand to her. For a second she hesitated, then placed her own in his. His grip was strong, and he pulled her to her feet with no difficulty at all. This was the first time she had touched the hand of a gentleman who was not wearing gloves.

* * *

Richard experienced an overwhelming desire to pull her into his arms and kiss her breathless, but thought it better not to do so. He had carefully avoided any mention of his intentions and had no wish to cause her to avoid him.

Her hand was not soft like other

young ladies', but as strong and firm as his own. He was about to release her when something prompted him to ask for answers to questions that had been bothering him.

'Freddie, how did my dogs come to be in your bedroom that night? And how the hell did you persuade my stallion to let you ride him?' He was still holding her hand, and felt her fingers tense. He didn't release her and she didn't pull away.

'I have a way with animals, Richard, and your horse decided that he liked me. When I took him out, your dogs joined us. If it hadn't been for them, I might have frozen to death whilst I hid in the hay barn waiting for an opportunity to put Othello back in his stable.'

'God's teeth! I had no idea you had been out all night. Small wonder you came down to find something hot to drink. I take it that the dogs followed you upstairs when you eventually came in?'

'I did not have the heart to refuse. They had lain on either side of me and kept me warm and deserved to be inside. From your expression, am I to understand that they do not come into the house as a rule?'

'They do not. However, I might now reconsider, as they have proved themselves to be more than just hunting dogs.' With some reluctance, he released his hold but remained close to her. 'Wolf and Smoke are as unsociable as my horse with every other person they have come in contact with. I have a bitch about to whelp; would you like to have the pick of the litter?'

Her eyes lit up and her smile was radiant. 'I should like nothing better. I have half a dozen spaniels at home, and have supplied most of the neighbourhood with puppies over the past three years. A hound would be a welcome addition to my pack.'

She turned as if to leave, but he didn't want her to go. 'Do you have a mare that my stallion could cover? His progeny make thousands of guineas at Tattersalls.'

What had possessed him to mention two taboo subjects, money and procreation? Neither were suitable topics of conversation with a young lady. To his surprise, she reacted as if this was nothing out of the ordinary.

'I have indeed got a mare who is the perfect age to foal. Should I send her to you when she is in season, or will you bring your stallion to us?'

'That can be decided nearer the time. If we don't retire immediately, we will be left in total darkness, as the wall sconces are about to gutter out.'

Freddie held her still burning candlestick aloft. 'Unlike you, I am fully prepared for such an eventuality. I intend to come down for breakfast; at what time are you intending for the treasure hunt to start?'

'The clues will be positioned as soon as my staff is up so the teams can begin their hunt whenever they wish. It continues until all the teams solve the last clue and come here with the items on the list.'

They were now in the grand hall. The candles here had been doused, but there was a glimmer of light coming from the huge log in the fireplace. This, according to Richard's mother, should not have been lit until Christmas Eve, but his aunt had wished to have it burning when the guests arrived.

He looked around appreciatively. The space smelled of cinnamon, nutmeg and Applewood, which gave it a festive feel. Fortuitously, Freddie had paused beneath the mistletoe.

'Forgive me, sweetheart, but if you do not wish to be kissed, you should not stand beneath a kissing bough.'

He slipped one arm around her waist to hold her still, and with his hand tilted her face. He pressed his mouth on hers. Her lips were cold and tasted sweet from the cake she had been eating. A surge of something he did not recognise flooded through him, and it took all his self-control not to turn a gentle kiss into one of passion.

Her response was not warm, but at least she had not recoiled from his touch. He had no intention of doing anything to alert her to the fact that he was determined to win her for himself. She was not in any way the sort of bride he had thought he would one day marry — but he was convinced she was the only woman who would suit him.

He dropped his arms and she nodded. 'I shall make certain I do not make such a mistake again. I find I am not overfond of being kissed.' She stared directly at him before continuing. 'I believe it might be different if one's feelings were engaged. I bid you good night, Richard, and shall see you in the morning.'

Before he could reply, she ran up the stairs and vanished into the guest wing. He followed more slowly, lost in thought. He had intended to speak to Mr Halston today, but now thought it might be advisable to leave things as they were. If Freddie heard from her father that he was pursuing her, she might well take umbrage.

Abingdon must be persuaded to hold his tongue on the matter as well — better not to alert Lucy either. Richard was convinced that it was only a matter of time before Freddie realised how lucky she was and would be eager to accept his proposal.

* * *

On her return, Freddie decided she was now tired enough to sleep, so put the novels on the side table in the parlour. She was woken by the rattle of curtains and the appetising smell of chocolate and sweet morning rolls.

'Good morning, miss. The snow has quite gone, but there's been a hard frost. What would you like me to put out for you today?'

'Something warm and with loose sleeves, but apart from that I shall leave the choice to you. Is my sister awake?'

'Polly has just taken in her tray.'

'In which case, would you be kind enough to take mine into the sitting room and ask Polly to do the same for my sister?'

Freddie scrambled out of bed and pulled on her dressing robe. She was aware that her maid was giving her strange glances, and realised she had seen the discarded garments from last night. It was none of the girl's business.

Lucy arrived a few minutes after her. 'You look much happier, dearest Freddie. Why is that? Is your arm no longer paining you?'

'It isn't, thank you, but that isn't the reason why I am in better spirits. I have decided to put aside my antipathy for Mr Finchley, and in future I shall be civil to him.' She had no intention of explaining to her sister why she had changed her view. 'After all, it is the time to be forgiving and loving to all mankind, is it not? There are many things about the man that I heartily dislike, but I intend to ignore those and get on with him in future.'

'I'm delighted to hear you say so. As long as I do not have to talk to him myself, I find him terrifying and prefer his cousin. Do not raise your eyebrows at me, Frederica; I do not have romantic feelings for him. There is another gentleman who has caught my attention, but I fear Mama will not allow him to approach me formally.'

'I take it that he is a brother of one of the other candidates and not a member of the aristocracy?'

'Actually, he is not. His name is Jonathan Rushton. His father is the second son of the Duke of Melbourne. By some wonderful coincidence, we are in the same team for the treasure hunt, which means we can spend all day in each other's company without causing comment.'

'I look forward to being introduced to him. I think it was rather high-handed of Mr Finchley to omit me from the list of names without asking my opinion. Don't look so worried, dearest; I shall not take him to task for it. Remember, from now on we shall be the best of friends.'

With an elegant russet-coloured velvet gown, and her hair arranged in a particularly becoming style, Freddie knew she had never looked better. Lucy was wearing velvet also, but her dress was in a deep blue which suited her fair colouring and exactly matched her eyes.

'I've just noticed, Freddie, that you have abandoned your sling altogether. Do you think it wise to do so?'

'I shall return to our apartment and put it on again if my arm begins to hurt. I wish to be able to eat my breakfast without the necessity of asking you to cut up my food as if I was a babe in leading strings.'

The handsome tall-case clock that stood to the left of the front door struck nine when they walked past on their way to the breakfast room. Freddie had expected to find the chamber fully occupied by other guests, but it was empty.

'I wonder where everyone is this morning? The party broke up relatively early last night, so I cannot think it is lack of sleep that is keeping people away.' Then they heard voices coming from the direction of the library.

Immediately, Lucy put down her plate and rushed to the door. 'Botheration! Some teams have already started — we are not early, but tardy. I must go in search of Mr Rushton.'

She rushed off, leaving Freddie alone. For the second time, she regretted not being part of the excitement. Then Finchley — she could not call him Richard in her thoughts, although she would do so to his face — strolled in. The smile he bestowed upon her made her toes curl in her slippers, which was a very uncomfortable sensation.

'Good morning, Freddie. Allow me to serve you. There are already three teams dashing about the place — I fear I shall regret arranging this treasure hunt by the time it is done.'

'I own that I did consider such a lively event not something you would enjoy.'

She saw something flash across his face, and if she didn't know better, she would have thought it regret.

'Do you think me such a stick in the mud? I can assure you that on one occasion I was known to enjoy myself.'

'That was probably several years ago, sir, as someone of your advanced years cannot be expected to do something so energetic as having fun.'

His rich, deep laugh filled the room. 'I'm not in my dotage, sweetheart. But perhaps eight and twenty must seem like Methuselah to someone just out of the schoolroom.'

He was irresistible when he was being charming, and she joined in his merriment. 'I shall be twenty years of age on my next name day, which is the fifth of January.'

'Shall you indeed? If I am honest, my dear, I had thought you considerably older.' He smiled as she pulled a face at his comment. 'I know, I cannot have it both ways. You have a maturity about you that is unusual for someone so young — I think that is why I enjoy your company.'

'I think that you prefer to be with me because you know I have no designs upon you. To the other young ladies present, I'm sure you are considered a very eligible bachelor.'

'I'm certain that they do. Now, enough of this nonsense. What do you wish me to bring you for your breakfast?'

She scarcely knew what she ate, but it was all tasty and she enjoyed it. They were unable to continue their banter, as they were joined by some of the older members of the party.

'My word, Finchley, you have opened Pandora's box. My dear wife is having a fit of the vapours at the misbehaviour she was obliged to witness,' an elderly bewhiskered gentleman told him firmly.

'It is harmless fun, my lord, and exactly what was needed to improve the atmosphere.'

Another spoke out, but this time in favour. Freddie quickly finished her plate and slipped away, as she felt uncomfortable being the only lady present.

Although she could not participate, she thought she would see for herself what was going on. She had warned Finchley that asking for a lady's garter might lead to trouble. A more pressing reason to absent herself was that she had no wish to be enticed to the attics by Finchley. He was larding his conversation with unnecessary endearments, and she had a nasty suspicion he had not given up on his pursuit of her despite the fact that she'd made her own position very clear.

10

Richard was unable to detach himself from the gentlemen speedily enough to prevent his quarry from vanishing. He was determined to make Freddie come to the attics in search of suitable gifts for the winners. The more time he spent in her company completely unchaperoned, the more likely it was that she would feel herself obliged to accept his offer.

He met his cousin in the passageway. 'I thought you would be with your team searching for clues, Abingdon.'

'I have been, but have come for sustenance. We are to take it in turns to eat so we will not fall behind. Do you know which team is in the ascendant at the moment?'

'I have no notion, but I intend to find out. I'm not sure that all the teams have started the hunt as yet. I left out seven sealed letters with the first clue — I'm going to the library to see how many are still there and which teams they are.'

'I cannot remember ever having had such a jolly time, Finchley. It is beginning to feel more like the festive period and less like a wake.'

As Richard had suspected, there were still two teams that had not yet begun the search. In order to progress with the hunt, each clue had to be solved. Once this was done, the team would discover the next sealed letter with their number upon it.

He was obliged to step aside as a fresh group of players rushed past to solve a puzzle. He checked the numbers against the lists of names and decided to send servants up to remind the participants they must get started if they wished to have a chance of winning.

The racket coming from the far end of the corridor must mean that some of the people had already solved the first three clues, as the fourth sent them to the orangery. The problem of the prizes had still to be resolved, so Richard set out in search of Freddie, determined to persuade her to come up to the attics. He was certain there were trunks of things that had come from India; his grandfather had visited that far-off country after Grandmama had died.

As far as Richard knew, no one had ever opened the boxes, so he had no idea what was inside. If there were bolts of Indian cloth, they would make ideal gifts for the young ladies. He followed the noise, and to his delight he discovered the very person he was searching for joining in the fun.

'Miss Halston, I have been looking for you. Would you be kind enough to spare me a few moments of your time?'

Reluctantly, she left the noisy crowd and followed him back to the library. 'I have no wish to go to the attics.'

'Not even to have first pick from several trunks of Indian items? There could be untold treasures, and I'm inviting you to come with me; we shall be the first to see them. Whatever you select shall be your name-day gift from the family.'

'I'm intrigued. How is it that no one ever looked inside the boxes?'

'My grandfather returned from his trip and was immediately struck down with the sweating sickness. These trunks arrived here several weeks after his death, and my parents consigned them to the attics as they brought back unhappy memories.'

'So they have stood up there unopened for many years?'

'Twenty years at least. Will you come with me?'

'I cannot resist the lure of Indian artefacts. Muslin, silk and cotton from that country are the height of fashion at the moment. Do you think your grandfather might have bought cloth?'

'I have no idea, and standing here discussing it will not reveal the answer. I have already sent a footman upstairs to unlock the doors and place oil lamps so we can see. There are windows at either end of each attic room, but there won't be much light at this time of year.'

Richard cared not what they would find; he had achieved his objective and was going to make the most of his opportunity. To reach the attics, one had to go past the nursery floor and then take a cramped and narrow staircase to the very top of the house.

Despite having an injured arm, Freddie negotiated the flights of stairs, so he did not get the opportunity to offer his assistance as he had hoped. The main door into these storage rooms had been wedged open.

She stopped so abruptly he cannoned into the back of her. Instinctively his arms shot out to grab the door frame — for a moment the matter hung in the balance as he teetered on the top step. Then he recovered and threw his weight forward.

* * *

Freddie received a second violent push and this time went head first over the trunk that had been left across the doorway. She was inches from a painful landing when Richard grabbed a handful of her bodice and heaved her upright. Hardly dignified, but it did the trick.

'I beg your pardon, sweetheart, for handling you so roughly.'

She pulled down the front of her gown and shook out the skirt before answering. 'And I apologise for almost causing you to fall backwards down the staircase and break your neck. However, as you can see, we were fortunate not to have been seriously hurt.' She pointed to the offending object. 'Why was this left so we could not fail to fall over it? Do you have a servant with a grudge?'

He lifted her out of the way and then took hold of the handle and dragged it to one side to join the other three that had been left in a more sensible position by the wall.

'As far as I'm aware, everyone in my employ is happy to be here. You can be very sure that I shall discover who the perpetrator of this idiocy is.'

The sound of running feet made them both turn to see who was arriving so precipitously. A red-faced young footman appeared, his half-wig askew, in the doorway. He took one look and clutched the door frame. If Finchley had not moved like lightning, the poor man would have tumbled backwards.

'Steady yourself and take a moment to recover your composure.'

The servant mopped his brow with his sleeve and eventually found the power of speech. 'I was going to bring the trunks downstairs, sir, but then thought I had better ask Mr Foster before I did so. I shouldn't have left that one where it was.'

Freddie's heart went out to him in his distress. He could well be dismissed without reference for such an error of judgement. She was about to intervene when her companion spoke.

'An honest mistake; I shall say no more about it.' He nodded towards the door, and the footman took off like a startled rabbit before Finchley could change his mind.

'I'm surprised you did not dismiss him — it's what I thought you would do.'

'If there had been an accident because of his carelessness, then matters would be different. Now, shall we open these treasure chests and see what my grandfather thought interesting enough to bring home with him?'

Freddie needed no second urging, and dropped to her knees beside the nearest box. She pushed back the locks and flung open the lid. 'Oh my! I've never seen anything so beautiful as these bolts of cloth. Look, there are shimmering silks in the most unusual colours, striped cottons and the finest muslin. One of these would make a perfect prize for a young lady.'

Richard knelt beside her and carefully lifted out the rolls of material, placing them in the centre of the attic room. There were at least two dozen, each one more stunning than the last.

'May I open the next one?'

'You do not have to ask my permission, my dear. Feel free to do as you please whilst under my roof.'

This was such a surprising statement that she sat back on her heels and stared at him, open-mouthed. 'Let me get this quite clear, Richard. I can behave exactly as I wish with your blessing?'

'I have just said so, sweetheart. Why do you question me like this?'

'I wished to be quite clear on this subject. I had not thought to enjoy myself whilst I was here, but now that I have your permission to do as I please, I believe things might be different.'

He looked wary, as well he might. 'You are twisting my words. You know exactly what I meant.'

'Too late to retract — you have given your promise. As soon as my arm is fully recovered, I intend to take your stallion out again. I shall also have your dogs sleep at the end of my bed, and I might even slide down the banister of the wooden staircase.'

There was a gleam in his eyes that she didn't like. He reached out and gently stroked her cheek with a finger covered in dust. 'You may have my hounds upstairs if you insist — but you will do either of the other things over my dead body.'

'I thought you to be an honourable gentleman, but I see I was sadly mistaken in the matter.' She shrugged and pouted like a silly chit, making it clear she had been teasing him.

His chuckle was infectious, and she could not help but join in. When he was in this sort of mood, she could almost like him.

'You are a baggage, my love, if you will forgive me for saying so.'

There was darkness in his eyes that disturbed her, and she hurriedly scrambled to her feet and rushed to the next trunk. If she was busy rummaging through the artefacts, he could not do anything reprehensible.

Each trunk was full of wonders: ivory carvings, silver ornaments of exotic figures, more bolts of silk, and in the last, an assortment of ivory and silver-topped walking canes.

'These will be ideal for the winning gentlemen so we have our prizes.' She held one up for his inspection.

'Let me see. Yes, the carving is exquisite. I've seen nothing like them before.'

Freddie was now filthy and cold, but well satisfied with their efforts. Richard reached down and assisted her to her feet. 'Come, my dear. You are half-frozen and have quite ruined your lovely gown. I should have allowed my staff to bring the trunks down so we could examine them in comfort.'

'I am well used to being both cold and dirty. I prefer to spend my time outside in all weathers. I abhor embroidery and other such ladylike pursuits.' She grinned up at him. 'But I do love to paint, and have my own studio at home.'

'Then you shall show your work to me when I come with Othello in the spring.'

'I should be pleased to do so. Please excuse me; I shall go to my rooms and repair the damage to my appearance that you have so kindly pointed out to me. If you are to take the prizes down, you must endeavour to keep them hidden from the participants — it would not do for them to know what they are to win.'

Richard viewed the two bolts of material and two walking sticks they had selected and sighed theatrically. 'I consider myself a resourceful gentleman, but even I cannot hide all this beneath my coat. Perhaps you have a solution to this conundrum?'

'But I shall certainly not put them under my skirt, so perhaps it would be best to leave them here and send a footman up to collect them.'

'I'm relieved to hear you say so,

sweetheart. I'm far too old and decrepit to indulge in silly games.' Richard was unused to conversing in this light-hearted manner, but was finding it most enjoyable. The more time he spent in Freddie's company, the more certain he was that he had made the right decision. Marriage to her would not be dull — in fact, he rather thought she would run him ragged.

They parted as they emerged from the nursery floor, but agreed to reconvene in his study when they had both removed the cobwebs and dirt from their clothes and persons.

It took but a minute for Richard's efficient valet to brush him down, and then all he had to do was complete his ablutions. He would be ready before her, and decided to arrange for refreshments to be served to them. He was ready for a pastry or two and a jug of coffee; and his beloved, he had noted, had a healthy appetite too. He could not abide a young lady who picked at her food and then, no doubt, devoured sweetmeats and cakes when out of sight.

The clues had been put about the downstairs rooms. It would have been a grave error of judgement to bring the young ladies and gentlemen to the bedroom floor. With hindsight, Richard regretted including the garter in the list of items to be scavenged, but there was nothing he could do about it.

He paused at the gallery and looked down into the hall. His home had never looked so welcoming, and he rather thought he would keep up the old traditions and have his house decorated for Christmastide every year. His mouth curved. Next year he hoped Freddie would be here as his wife, and she could make the decision for him.

The atmosphere at Finchley Hall was different — even his staff were going about their business with a spring in their step and a smile on their face. He was obliged to move aside as an eager team raced past him, presumably looking for the clue that would be found in the boot room.

He snapped his fingers and gave his order and then strolled in the direction of his study. As the instigator of this hunt, he thought it behoved him to check that all the teams were now active, so he had best visit the library first.

The last two papers had gone, so all the teams were now racing about the place. The final clue would lead them back to the library, but he doubted any of them would have solved and collected everything before the afternoon.

The sun was shining, albeit weakly, and the ornamental lake was frozen solid. He would invite Freddie to accompany him there so they could investigate together if the ice was thick enough to skate on. It was years since he had indulged in this frivolous pastime, but he rather thought he would enjoy spinning about the ice if he had Freddie in his arms.

The coffee and cakes arrived before

she did. He dismissed the footman who had brought them and poured some of the bitter aromatic brew into two cups ready for her arrival. He did not have long to wait, as she rushed in.

'Am I tardy? I'm normally known for my punctuality.' She flashed him a brilliant smile and helped herself to pastries. 'It is pandemonium out there. I doubt that the older generation will approve of so much excitement and exercise.'

'Hopefully both sides will band together in their opprobrium, and then my mission will be complete. When we are done here, I wondered if you would like to come with me and see if the ice is hard enough to skate on.'

'I should love to. A brisk walk across the park is exactly what I need. I wish that the doctor would come back and remove the sutures today. I heal far quicker than most people and I believe they could come out now.'

'The housekeeper is adept at such things. She takes care of my staff, and we rarely have the need to call in a physician. Why not get her to do it for you? Then you will not have to wait until after Christmas for his return.'

'I shall do so when we get back from our walk. I am not a proficient skater; I am more likely to fall than glide.'

'I, of course, am an expert. It would be an honour to teach you, if you will allow me to do so?'

She choked, inelegantly spraying crumbs across the room. 'An honour? It will be a penance, Richard, as the only activity that I am good at is riding. On the two attempts that I tried to skate, my feet insisted in going in opposite directions despite the best efforts of those designated to teach me. My sister is far better at skating and dancing.'

'Shall we have a wager, sweetheart? If I cannot teach you to skate, then I shall pay a forfeit of your choice. If I am successful, then you shall be the one to pay a forfeit.'

She tilted her head and gave him a direct look. 'I do not normally approve of gambling, but as we are not to participate in the noisy fun outside this chamber, I think it only fair we can indulge in something a little reprehensible. Therefore, I take the challenge.'

11

On her return from donning her boots and cloak, Freddie spotted her sister in the passageway. She was accompanied by a handsome young gentleman who must be the one of whom she was speaking so fondly.

'Freddie, this is Mr Rushton.'

This was rather an informal introduction, but in the circumstances it would suffice. She nodded and he did the same. There was something she did not quite like about him. She could not put her finger on it, but thought there was something hard in his eyes that should not be there in one so young.

Lucy seemed unaware of any tension. 'We have been sent in search of a black feather, and have no idea where we might find one. We have investigated several cushions and pillows and they all have been filled with goose down.'

'I think you might be better looking in the barnyard. I'm certain I heard a cockerel crowing this morning, and they always have black tail feathers.'

Lucy squealed with delight. 'Quickly — we must get on our outdoor garments and go in search of the missing object. Are you going out as well?'

'I'm going with Mr Finchley to see if we can skate on the lake tomorrow.' She had thought her sister might raise an eyebrow at her choice of companion, but Lucy was already scampering upstairs, pursued by Mr Rushton, and had forgotten her. She frowned as she watched them go and decided she would make some enquiries about this young man.

Whilst she waited, Freddie wandered around the huge hall examining the garlands in more detail. She was particularly careful to avoid the central chandelier with the kissing bough dangling beneath it. There was not long to wait as Finchley arrived, magnificent in a many-caped greatcoat, a tall beaver on his head and his gloves in his hand.

'We must exit through a side door, my dear, as it leads directly to the path we need to take to the lake. I've sent a message to Bevan, and she will be ready to attend to you whenever you send for her.'

A lurking footman was already at the door and held it open for them. Freddie's companion offered his arm, and she slipped hers through it. The path was treacherous, and she had no wish to twist her ankle in a fall.

'Forgive me for asking, but how many footmen do you employ? We have six, and I think that more than enough even for such a large establishment as ours. I surmise that you have three times that number.'

'To be honest, I leave such matters to my mother. We have far more servants than we need, but if I did not employ them they might well end up in the poorhouse. Life is difficult for those less fortunate than ourselves. Not all land-lords take care of their people as we do.'

'Papa is of the same mind. However,

Mama refuses to have more than six male staff, plus the butler, but we have double the amount of maids that we need. Outside it is different — one cannot move without falling over a gardener, stable boy or some such person.'

Once they were on the grass, she released her hold, as she was sure she would not slip. Richard adjusted his long stride to hers. They had not gone more than a few yards when Smoke and Wolf joined them.

'You have your master's permission to sleep inside with me, boys, but somehow I think you would prefer to be in the stables as usual.' She patted each grey head and they gambolled around her, obviously delighted to be with them.

'My dogs like nothing better than fetching a stick,' she said. 'I suppose that would be beneath your dogs?'

'They are hunters; they will catch you a rabbit or a deer, but I doubt they would fetch you a stick. Shall we try?'

He picked up a branch that had been blown from the woods they were walking beside and broke a suitable piece from it, then hurled it across the frosty grass; and to their shock, the hounds raced after it barking in excitement.

'How extraordinary! It never occurred to me that a hound would want to retrieve.'

Freddie pointed as Wolf snatched up the wood and raced back to them, with Smoke beside him trying to wrench it from his jaws.

'Good boys, well done. Drop it now.' Instead of doing as requested by their master, the hounds continued to run in circles around them, and obviously had no intention of giving up their prize.

'They are enjoying themselves, but I fear they will not relinquish the stick however much you ask them to.'

He scooped up a second one and threw it an impressive distance. Again, they dashed off, and this time Smoke picked it up.

'At least they are getting plenty of exercise,' Freddie told her companion as they arrived at the edge of the water. 'How are you going to test if the ice is safe?'

'Like this.' He stepped onto the lake and proceeded to jump up and down.

She wasn't sure if she was impressed or shocked by his disregard for danger. Fortunately, the ice didn't crack and he returned to her side unscathed.

★   ★   ★

Richard had known before he stepped onto the ice that it would be perfectly safe to do so. It was obvious from the opaque colour that the water was probably solid to the bottom. Even if he had gone through, it would have been no more than embarrassing and cold as the lake was no more than a few feet deep even in the middle.

'That was a foolhardy thing to do, Richard, and the sort of behaviour I might have expected from a schoolboy, not a sensible gentleman like yourself.'

'Would you like to have your first

attempt at skating now? I merely have to wave an arm and someone will run out here with the necessary blades.'

'You are ridiculous, sir, and I refuse to join in your nonsense. Would I be right in thinking you do not have enough skates for every member of the party who wishes to go on the ice?'

'Of course I do not. Why should I keep two dozen pairs of skates when there are only half a dozen members of my family?' He held out his hands. 'The ice is safe, sweetheart. Allow me to show you how to move on it without coming to grief.'

She hesitated but then placed her gloves in his. 'Actually, I think I might prefer to be on the ice without blades.'

He guided her safely onto the frozen water. 'Move each foot smoothly and don't lift it from the ice. Do what I am doing.'

She snorted and pulled a face. 'As you are going backwards, that is a ridiculous suggestion.'

'How observant of you, my love, I

had not noticed that myself.' He exerted a little more pressure on her hands. 'Mirror my movements, but in reverse, of course.'

She did as he asked, and soon they were moving at some speed along the edge of the lake. All might have been well if his dogs, which they had both forgotten about, had not chosen to join them. Naturally enough, as soon as they bounded onto the ice, their legs spreadeagled and they skidded across the surface, barking wildly.

Richard attempted to pull them both aside but failed miserably. The dogs collided with their legs, and despite his best efforts to stay upright, he tumbled backwards, taking Freddie with him. He landed on his back, grateful he had had the foresight to wear his coat, which protected him from serious hurt.

As he had kept hold of Freddie, his body cushioned her fall, so she too was safe from injury. Although the ice was thick, it could not take the double weight of them both falling from such a height and with such force. There was an ominous cracking, and they were both engulfed in icy water. Obviously, his premise had been wrong — the lake has not been completely frozen.

The water wasn't deep, and Richard managed to keep his feet under him and his arms tightly around Freddie. They were not totally submerged, but only to their waists, in the lake. The weight of his heavy greatcoat was now a hindrance, and she must be having the same problem with her skirts.

'Do you think if you waved your arm, someone might come out and help us?' Despite the appalling situation they were in, she still was able to jest. She was a remarkable young woman — like no one he had ever met before.

'I think, sweetheart, I can extricate us without involving my servants. If you would care to put your arms around my neck instead of my waist, I shall soon have us out of here.'

She did as he instructed, and he waded the two steps necessary to take them to the bank and then swung her to safety. He had expected her to move away, but instead she leaned down and offered her hand to help him scramble out.

He was loath to take it, as he was a big man and he had no wish to tip her head first back into the freezing lake. 'Take hold, Richard, and do not be ridiculous. I am stronger than I look.'

As he could no longer feel his extremities, and his best boots were ruined, he decided to do as she asked. She pulled and he managed to get one knee on the edge and then he was face first in the mud surrounded by a pool of water.

He rolled into a sitting position, and was about to pull off his boots and empty them, but Freddie was there before him. 'Allow me. The sooner we both get inside and into dry clothes, the better. I've no wish to catch a congestion of the lungs after this adventure.'

Whilst she pulled off one boot, Richard did the same for the other.

Once they were emptied, he pulled them on again and sprung to his feet.

'Take my hand, sweetheart, and we shall run back. It will get our circulation moving and restore much-needed warmth to our limbs.'

Through chattering teeth, she answered, 'I fear that your plan to have skating tomorrow might well be quite spoilt after our excitement.' Then her expression changed to alarm. 'Your dogs — where arc they?'

'God damn it! I had quite forgotten them.' They both spun around, and to his relief, both animals were at that very moment scrabbling onto dry land. They were wet, but unharmed by their unexpected swim. 'Smoke, Wolf, come.'

He broke into a run, almost dragging Freddie alongside until she was able to continue under her own volition. The dogs were beside them all the way to the house. He had expected to be obliged to summon assistance, but the side door was open and servants were waiting with blankets to receive them.

He had no need to ask for his dogs to be taken care of, as two stable boys were there to lead them away to be dried.

The housekeeper had her arm around Freddie's waist and was bustling her up the secondary staircase. Richard followed behind, his feet squelching unpleasantly in his waterlogged boots. He had already tossed his sodden greatcoat to a footman, and no doubt it would be returned to him by the morrow in its usual pristine state.

He caught up with Freddie. 'I'm sure there will be a hot bath waiting for us both. When you are fully recovered, I shall come and speak to you in your sitting room.'

★　★　★

Freddie was beginning to take for granted the fact that her every whim was catered for without her having to ask. She stripped off her sodden garments unaided and stepped into the lemon-scented water with relief.

'What shall I put out for you, miss?' Mary asked.

'As long as it is warm, I care not. The housekeeper is coming to remove my stitches — or at least to see if they can come out a few days early.'

Her maid handed her a washcloth. 'The cut has healed already and there's no redness. I don't think you will have a scar at all.'

She gently wiped the cloth over the injury and felt no pain. The only problem was that the stitches pulled uncomfortably when she moved her arm. Once they were gone, she would be able to wear her evening gowns and join in the jollity. Whatever her host said, there was no chance of her attempting to skate. The wager would have to be considered void.

'I shall remain in my undergarments until my arm has been dealt with, Mary.'

Bevan arrived with silver scissors and carefully snipped the sutures. 'The doctor did a good job of his sewing, Miss Halston; almost as neat as I would have done.'

'Thank you. If I had known you were proficient in this area, I should have been happy to allow you to attend to me. So far I have been here four days and had two accidents; I sincerely hope your skills will not be called on for a third one.'

'With all the goings-on with this treasure hunt, miss, I shouldn't be surprised if there are several accidents before it's done.' The housekeeper curtsied and departed.

The gown that her maid had selected for her was in a becoming shade of gold with long sleeves, no rouleaux or ruffles anywhere, and a matching spencer. She was just ready when her visitor arrived in the sitting room.

'You have timed it perfectly, sir, but I'm at a loss to know why you wished to speak to me so urgently that you have come here and not waited until I was available downstairs.' Freddie could not prevent her smile.

As always, Richard looked the epitome of a rich gentleman. His topcoat was dark green, his waistcoat a lighter hue of the same colour, and at his neck was a froth of complicated cotton. She spoke without thinking. 'I see you favour the more elaborate style of neckcloth — would that be a waterfall?' 'I've no idea — I leave such matters to my valet. Is it not to your taste? It is a little flamboyant for me.' 'You have not answered my first question, as to why you are here.'

He didn't answer and appeared to be listening to something. Then he strode to the door and opened it, and a footman came in with the prizes. 'Put them on the window seat.' The man did as he was told and scurried off. 'I thought it would be best to have them here where no one is likely to find them.'

'You forget that my sister shares this room with me and could return at any moment. We must put them in my bedchamber.'

His expression of incredulity made her

giggle. 'Botheration! I should not have suggested we go into my bedchamber. My maid can hide them for us. There's no need to look so scandalised.'

Once Freddie had given her instructions to her maid, she was about to accompany him when she remembered her disquiet about the gentleman her sister appeared to favour. 'What do you know about the Rushton family? My sister thinks your cousin eligible, but I cannot like him. All I know is that his grandfather is the Duke of Melbourne.'

'I cannot tell you anything about him as they are friends of my aunt. I shall make enquiries and get back to you. My cousin has every intention of making your sister an offer if ever knowledge of our being together at that hostelry becomes public.'

'As I explained to you before, there is absolutely no need for you to concern yourselves about our reputations. We shall be gone from your toplofty echelons soon enough and you will be able to forget about us.'

'That I could never do. You are an original, sweetheart, and I have no intention of allowing you to disappear from my life.'

She was about to protest at this statement, but he opened the sitting-room door and all but pushed her through it. A discussion of such personal matters could hardly take place in the corridor, so she must hold her tongue until they were private again.

Three overexcited young ladies flew across the hall and vanished down the corridor she had not as yet explored. They were halfway when a second group rushed across travelling in the opposite direction. On both occasions she and her companion were forced to leap aside in order to avoid being bowled over.

'There are people in the drawing room now; I think it might be wise if I joined them. I do not wish to create any further speculation that might link our names together.'

He nodded. 'I shall complete the investigation myself and come and find you when I have anything pertinent to say.'

Freddie was greeted by her mother, who was sitting with two of the matrons from the grand side of the house party. 'Frederica, I have not seen you for an age. I am so relieved that you are not participating in this ridiculous treasure hunt. Lady Tewkesbury, allow me to introduce you to my oldest daughter.'

Freddie curtsied and received a brief nod in response. Her mother then completed the introductions.

'Frederica, make your curtsy to Lady Avon.'

This time the response was warmer and included a gesture that she join the group. Once she was settled, all three looked at her expectantly.

'I have had the most exciting time, Mama, which ended with me falling through the ice on the lake.'

She related the story, and all three were laughing when she had completed it. They discussed the rackety behaviour of some of the young ladies and gentlemen, and she sympathised with their concerns.

'Mr Finchley wished his guests to get to know each other, and he has certainly achieved his aims. The winners will be announced and the prizes given after dinner this evening. This will be the first time I have joined the company and I cannot wait.'

Lady Tewkesbury actually smiled at her. 'Your unfortunate incident with the fish has pleased dear Lord Tewkesbury. He has been trying to entice Mr Finchley's French chef away, and now he has him. For myself, I prefer to see what I am eating, but his lordship prefers the French style of cooking.'

'Are we to go to church at midnight, do you know?'

'It's too far away to travel at night, Miss Halston,' Lady Avon explained. 'I am sure that we shall go to matins on Christmas Day as long as the weather allows. The countess told me the curate will come here to conduct a service if we cannot attend ourselves.'

Her mother tapped her on the arm. 'I think that Mr Finchley wishes to speak to you, Frederica.'

She glanced across the room, and he was indeed lurking in the doorway. She nodded and he vanished hastily before he could be called over to converse with the three ladies.

'Please excuse me; I am helping Mr Finchley with the organisation of the treasure hunt.'

He was lounging against the wall just out of sight when she emerged. 'I had no intention of coming in to fetch you, so it is a good thing your mother saw me.'

'You did it on purpose — you wish there to be gossip about us. I cannot imagine why, as you know my opinion on the matter.'

Richard appeared unbothered by her reprimand. The disturbing glint in his eye was worse than his knowing smile.

'I have discovered quite a lot about Rushton,' he said, 'and none of it pleases me.'

'He comes from a good family and is obviously wealthy, so what is it about him that displeases you?'

'His family are wealthy, that's true. But he is a hardened gambler and has a reputation for being a rake. I think he has made up his mind to ensnare your sister with his charm and force her into a marriage to obtain access to her fortune.'

'I must find them and rescue her before something untoward takes place.'

'We shall find them together, Freddie, but then you must take Lucy away and leave me to deal with him.'

'You can hardly evict him from your home the day before Christmas, as that would mean his family have to go as well.'

A shiver of apprehension ran down her spine when she saw his face. He had changed from an amiable companion to a formidable stranger. She would not wish to be Rushton when Finchley found him.

Most of the teams had now completed more than half of the clues and collected most of the items they needed to finish the hunt. This meant that they were all rushing about in the main reception rooms, where any young lady would be safe enough from unwanted advances.

They had been searching for over half an hour and still not come across Lucy or Rushton. 'I have a very bad feeling about this, Richard. I can think of only one reason why they should both be absent.' The earl wandered by, looking slightly dishevelled but perfectly content to be so. When he heard the reason they wanted Rushton and Lucy, he became as fierce as his cousin.

'Freddie, you must leave this to us now. Return to the drawing room and remain there until I send word for you.' She nodded and blinked back unwanted tears. His expression softened, and he moved closer so he could speak to her without being overheard.

'Don't look so worried, my love. I give you my word everything will be all right. Do you trust me?'

'I do, of course I do.' If anyone could save her sister from ruin, it was these two gentlemen.

'I have no wish to be questioned by the ladies taking tea in the drawing room,' said Richard, 'so I shall wait in the library. There should be teams finishing the quest, and I can collect their answers and items and put them somewhere safe.'

'Very well. I shall find you there.'

12

As soon as Freddie was safe in the library, Richard turned to Abingdon. 'I have a bad feeling about this, my friend. I think we are more likely to find them in a bedchamber than anywhere else.'

'If that bastard has violated her, I will break his neck.'

'You will do no such thing. You would be dangling from a rope if you did so.'

'She is a sweet, innocent young lady and does not deserve — '

'No lady deserves to be mistreated in that way. He will not have taken her to any of the rooms that are in use, so we shall start with those that are set aside for visiting governesses and senior servants.'

'If we separate, we shall find them quicker. I give you my word, I will not harm him but escort him to your study, where you can deal with the matter as you see fit.'

Richard knew that to race about the place would draw attention, so he walked briskly, even pausing to exchange a brief word with an older gentleman on his way to play billiards. The first room he looked in was cold and dark and obviously hadn't been occupied for some time. When he approached the second, the unmistakable sound of movement told him he had been correct.

In two strides, he reached the door and flung it open, deliberately making it crash against the wall. He stood immobile for a second, unable to believe what he was seeing. Lucy was standing over Rushton's unconscious body, a candlestick in one hand.

'Oh, I am so glad you have come in search of us. I fear I might have killed this man, as I struck him harder than I intended.'

'Whatever you did, my dear, I'm sure that he deserved it.' Richard walked smoothly to her side and gently prised the candlestick from her clenched fingers. 'Are you unhurt?'

He didn't need to elaborate, as she understood immediately to what he was inferring. 'Apart from my dignity, I am perfectly well. I was bamboozled by his charm into thinking he was a pleasant gentleman when the reverse was the case.'

Richard dropped to one knee and checked there was a pulse. He found it, weak but regular. There was a prodigious amount of blood seeping from a head wound, and this needed immediate attention. Richard was going to remove his neckcloth, but from the sound of ripping material, Lucy was already tearing strips from her petticoat.

'Here — when one of the grooms had a similar injury, I remember that a pad was put on the wound and then tied into place.'

She didn't offer to help with the bandaging, but he was capable of doing this himself. He had just tied the ends of the makeshift bandage when Abingdon rushed in.

'I thought I heard voices. God's teeth! I thought we agreed we would not kill him.'

'I beg your pardon, my lord — it was not Mr Finchley who rendered this villain unconscious, but me. He lured me here saying this was where we would discover the answer to a clue, and then . . . '

'There is no need to say any more, Miss Lucy; we know exactly what sort of person this object is,' said Abingdon. He pointed to the door. 'Why don't you retire to your apartment and allow us to deal with this matter?'

'Thank you; I shall do that.' She headed for the door but stopped to speak again before she left. 'I'm not in the habit of violence, but that vile man intended to force me into marriage by having us discovered in here together.' She didn't wait to hear their response.

'That means he must have an accomplice in this scheme,' Richard deduced. 'Give me a hand to put him on the bed.'

'Do you intend to send for the doctor?' Abingdon asked.

'No, I shall get Bevan to take care of him.' He took the shoulders and his cousin took the feet, and together they heaved the unconscious form onto the bed. There was a large pool of blood on the boards which needed cleaning if it wasn't to be a permanent reminder of what had taken place here.

'We need to come up with a reasonable explanation for how Rushton has been injured,' Richard said. 'I suggest that we say he was searching for a clue and tripped and hit his head on something.' He looked around. 'He could have received a head wound if he had fallen against the corner of the fireplace.'

There was a small strip of unused petticoat on the floor. Quickly he dipped it in the gore and smeared some on the corner of the mantelshelf.

'That's all very well, Finchley, but how are we to explain our presence here? Also, the fact that we have dealt with his wound will not go unnoticed.'

'More to the point, there could well be someone coming to supposedly discover Lucy and Rushton in a compromising position.' He thought for a moment and then came to a decision. 'Would you go downstairs and fetch Bevan? If she is here attending to him, then that will be one problem solved.'

It might have been better to have left the bastard where he was and done nothing to stem the bleeding, but then they might have a corpse on their hands instead of an unconscious man. They must just hope the housekeeper would be here first.

Richard closed the door and saw there was a bolt, which he pushed across. This would keep out unwanted visitors, but it would not solve the problem of how to come up with a reasonable explanation. The crony, whoever he was, would be coming in the expectation of finding Freddie's sister hopelessly compromised. The fact that she was no longer there would not help the situation, as the unconscious gentleman would no doubt be only too happy to regale to anyone who was prepared to listen the fact that he had been alone with a willing partner in an unoccupied bedchamber. All Rushton needed to say was that Lucy had come willingly but then had a change of heart and struck him down. He would appear to be the innocent party, and she and her family would be ruined. Freddie was under a misapprehension if she thought such a scandal would not follow them.

A faint groan from the bed alerted Richard to the fact that the scoundrel was coming around. Somehow he had to persuade this morally corrupt man to do the right thing. There was only one way out of this dilemma, and it wasn't one he was happy about — but he had no choice if he was to protect the good name of the Halston family.

★ ★ ★

Freddie was kept busy, as there was already a team solving the final clue in the library. She put the answers and the objects in a pile and tied them neatly with a ribbon.

'Mr Finchley and I will check the answers when we have got them all here. You will note that I have put the time of your arrival and initialled it, so there can be no dispute that you were first back.'

'Then we are the winners,' a gentleman with shirt points so high he could not turn his head, and a lurid purple and yellow waistcoat, announced.

'You might very well be, but it is possible you have some incorrect answers and do not have all the items specified. Therefore, the winners will be those who were first to return with everything in order. They will be announced after dinner tonight.'

One of the slightly dishevelled young ladies giggled. 'I've never had so much fun in my entire life, Miss Halston. Are we to know what the winners receive as a prize? Or is that also to be kept secret until after dinner?'

'I can only tell you that whoever wins will be delighted with what they receive.'

The four of them wandered off to repair their disarray, and then had agreed to meet in the music room, where a game of charades was to be played. How this had been arranged when all the young people had been dashing about the place, Freddie had no idea, but was glad the house party was now a lively affair. She was not overfond of playing games of any sort herself, but her sister would enjoy participating.

It had been more than an hour since Finchley and the earl had gone in search of Lucy. As there had been no word, she did not know how matters stood. The passageway was quiet; it had taken the last group a good half an hour to find the final clue, so she had ample time to run upstairs and see if her sister had returned safely.

On entering the sitting room, she found Lucy emerging from the bedchamber in a fresh gown. 'I'm so glad you are here, Freddie dearest. I have had such a horrible experience.'

When the sorry story unfolded, Freddie was horrified and angry in equal measure. 'I think we must both go on as if nothing out of the ordinary had transpired, my love, and you shall help me in the library as the teams finish the hunt.'

'I think that the other gentleman in our group was not of the same ilk as Rushton, and Priscilla is so featherbrained she could not possibly have been part of it.'

'Then you have nothing to worry about. It will be better for you to be seen happy and enjoying yourself just in case that scoundrel tries to blacken your name.'

The time arrived to change for dinner, and still Finchley had not sent word to her. All the teams had returned, some with more success than others, but all having enjoyed the experience. Lucy appeared to have put her fears aside and had left to join the charades party very soon after coming to the library.

Freddie wasn't sure if she should remain where she was until Richard came, or do as the others and retire. She wished to look her best tonight, as she hadn't been seen in the evenings since the disastrous first night.

Then he arrived, and she couldn't tell from his demeanour how things had gone. 'I have been anxious — why didn't you come to me before this?'

He glanced over his shoulder and then closed the door behind him. 'Things were a little more complicated than I had anticipated. Please be seated whilst I explain what has happened and how I have dealt with it.'

'I already know what happened to my sister and what she did — she has fully recovered from her unpleasant experience and has spent most of the afternoon playing silly games with the others. I'm certain no one will suspect she has been involved in anything untoward.'

'Excellent — I knew I could rely on you to step forward even if you hadn't heard from me. I shall tell you what has been done. Rushton had arranged for one of his friends to burst in on him and your sister, but fortunately she had gone before then.'

'I had not considered anyone else would be embroiled in this nasty business. That changes everything.'

'I see you understand exactly the predicament I was in. I was able to talk to Rushton before anyone else arrived, and the matter has been settled satisfactorily. He will say he fell and hit his head while searching for a clue, and that he had been in his cups when he suggested to his friend that he intended to seduce your sister.'

'Are he and his family to remain, or are you sending them away?'

'I have had him transferred to his chamber, and he will remain there until two days after Christmas, when he and his family will leave. They were not involved in his scheme, so I have no wish to cause them any more embarrassment than they must feel by being associated with such a man.'

'My sister and I owe you and the earl a debt of gratitude. I shall now retract and apologise for the epithets I applied to you when we first met. I no longer consider you anything but an honourable and pleasant gentleman.'

'Then we shall say no more about it, sweetheart. I see you have the results neatly parcelled. Have you had time to check the answers?'

'I have ticked off the items — the team that arrived first was short on two things, but all the rest have managed to collect everything. However, as I have no idea of the answers to your riddles, you must do that yourself.'

'If I call them out, we can do it together. It should not take more than a few minutes.'

It turned out that the second team

were in fact the victors. 'I shall get my maid to take the prizes to the drawing room whilst we are dining,' Freddie said. 'I must go or I shall be tardy. I have no wish to offend my host, as he is a most irascible gentleman and would give me the most horrible set-down.'

His laughter followed her down the passageway, and she all but skipped into her bedchamber to get ready.

13

Richard sauntered to his apartment in better spirits than he had been — well, than he had ever been, if he was honest. Despite the inauspicious beginning to this festive period, he was now a fair way to actually enjoying having the house full. This was due entirely to Freddie. As his feelings for her had changed, so had his outlook on many other things.

She had been correct to call him high in the instep, arrogant and disdainful — but all that was behind him. He had been brought up to think he was a superior being purely by the happenstance of his birth. The man who had tried to seduce Lucy was from one of the most prestigious families in the country and had behaved in the most despicable way.

How could he have been so blind? It was not a matter of birth that decided what sort of person one was, but how one behaved.

He had every intention of marrying his darling Freddie, whatever she might think about the matter; and what better day to propose than Christmas Eve? He would wait until after the presentation to the winners and then whisk her away somewhere private to make his offer.

The usual practice was for the hopeful suitor to speak to the young lady's father before addressing her, but he thought with Freddie it might be sensible to do it the other way round. Once her parents knew he was interested, they would put undue pressure on their daughter to accept him, and he wanted to be sure the decision was hers alone.

His evening clothes were waiting for him, and it did not take him more than a few minutes to get ready; or to be more accurate, for his valet to prepare him. He heard his female cousins going past, and they were more animated than usual. They were usually quiet ladies, not like their brother at all.

As Richard strolled along the passage-way, it occurred to him that he ought to have a betrothal ring to present when he made his offer. His mother kept the family jewellery in a safe in her apart-ment, and he could hardly ask her to find him something suitable, as then she would be cognisant of his plans.

He paused to lean his elbows on the balustrade and gaze down into the gal-lery. Already there were several people wandering about enjoying the atmosphere. As he watched, the oldest son of Lord Southwark stole a kiss from his compan-ion. It was a chaste kiss, a mere brush of the lips on her cheek, but it was enough to send the young lady into overexcited giggles.

That was where he would propose to Freddie. Somehow he would lure her under the chandelier and then be able to kiss her when she accepted. He wouldn't contemplate the awful thought that she would continue to refuse him, as they were now good friends.

Abingdon joined him. 'Even though I have abandoned my cork-brained scheme to sell my title to the highest bidder, this has turned out to be a most delightful Christmas. I cannot remember the house ever being so jolly. I believe that even you might have warmed to this house party.'

'I have indeed, my friend, and I intend to do the same every year. We had better join our guests; it would seem uncivil if both of us are missing from the drawing room.'

He saw immediately that Freddie had not yet come down, and neither had her sister, but Mrs Halston and her husband were there. They were chatting to Lord and Lady Southwark as if they were bosom beaux. As these two were about to become his in-laws, he was pleased they were considered acceptable by his friends.

From a distance, he heard his beloved laughing, and he immediately moved into the shadows of the doorway so he could watch her descending the marble staircase without being observed himself. When he had first seen her, he had thought her passable but not in any way remarkable.

The woman who was running lightly downstairs, the loop of material that held up the train of her evening gown over one wrist, her reticule in the other hand, was an incomparable. Freddie was taller than most women, but carried herself like a queen. Tonight she had her hair arranged in an elaborate style with what looked like pearls threaded through it. Her gown was ivory silk that flowed and shimmered as she moved, revealing a golden underskirt.

Richard scarcely noticed her sister, although he had thought her a lovely young lady when he had first set eyes on her. He had never seen anything so beautiful in his life as the young woman he intended to marry at the earliest possible opportunity. He carefully schooled his features so he would not reveal his feelings and give her an opportunity to avoid him.

Richard bowed as she approached and curtsied. 'Good evening, Miss Halston, Miss Lucy. Might I be permitted to say that you both look quite enchanting?'

Her smile was radiant. 'Thank you, and might I be permitted to return the compliment? Black suits you and makes you look even taller.'

He could hardly offer his arm, as it would mean her sister walked unescorted, so he stepped aside and then followed them in. Every gentleman present stopped what they were doing in order to stare appreciatively. He was not the only one who thought these two were diamonds of the first water.

* * *

Freddie tried to ignore the gentleman walking rather too close behind her, but for some strange reason, every time she was within his arm's reach she was uncomfortable; this was not something she was familiar with.

'Lucy, Mama is beckoning to us. We

have no alternative but to join them and be introduced to their new acquaintances.'

After spending the required few minutes, Freddie drifted away, leaving her sister to escape how best she could. She moved to an inconspicuous place behind a marble pillar and viewed the assembled company more closely.

'Do not look so concerned, sweetheart. I can assure you that any attention you are attracting tonight is because you are *ravissante*.'

She attempted to look disapproving. 'I wish you would not creep up on a person as you do, Finchley. It is most disconcerting.'

'I aim to please, my love. Foster is about to announce that dinner is served. Tonight you will go in on my arm. I will brook no argument on that score.'

He was smiling down at her in a most particular way, and her bodice became unaccountably tight. 'I should be delighted to do so, sir, as I would much prefer to talk to you than anyone else.' Something flashed across his face, and she thought it might be pleasure at her comment, but she dismissed this as a fanciful idea.

'I enjoy your company too, my dear, as I never know what outrageous remark you're going to make next.'

He whisked her to the front of the milling crowd; they entered first, and he escorted her to the head of the table. Waiting footmen pulled out the chairs and sat them as if they were royalty. How things had changed in the past few days — the families from both sides of society now were intermingled and apparently quite happy with the new arrangement. The jollity echoing from the other dining room meant whoever was in there was equally content with the arrangements.

'Everyone seems happy tonight,' Freddie remarked. 'I cannot credit what a difference holding that treasure hunt has made to your house party. Not only are the two groups pleased to be together, but also there is now no divide between the younger and older generation.'

'I think perhaps that things have moved too far in the other direction. It is, after all, the eve of the birth of our Lord, and perhaps the mood should be more serious.'

'Fiddlesticks to that! This day has been a celebration since pagan times — those who followed the old religions celebrated the fact that from today the nights will get shorter and the days longer.'

'My word! Could it be that I am sitting next to a heathen?' Richard's expression was stern, but his eyes were laughing at her.

'It would serve you right if I said that I am a white witch, Finchley. I am a good Christian like everyone else at this table.'

He turned his head slightly so that he could speak directly to her for fear of being overheard. 'I beg to dispute that, sweetheart. A Christian, certainly — but good? I wonder if that is true.'

The first course was set out down the centre of the table and it all looked quite delicious. 'If you are to serve me, then as long as it is not fish of any description, I will have a little of everything.'

'Fish is no longer served, so you are safe to eat whatever you like.'

Had Richard done this just for her? She could think of no other reason why he should have made such a drastic change to his menu. 'I think it's unfair that the rest of your guests should be deprived of something that they enjoy. Perhaps tomorrow you could arrange for anything fish-related to be placed at the far end of the table so that I am unlikely to taste it by mistake.'

'That would be an excellent notion, my dear, if I could be certain you and I would be sitting in the same places as we are now. I cannot always barge to the front — my mother has always preferred to let guests find their own positions.'

He was careful not to monopolise her, and she chatted to a pleasant lady to the right of her. When the final cover was removed, Mrs Finchley rose gracefully, and this was the sign for all the other ladies to follow and leave the gentlemen to their port.

She was waylaid by two young ladies she had been introduced to, but could not recall their names. 'Miss Halston, do you know who has won? Do you know what the prizes are to be?'

'I do, but I have no intention of revealing this information. Mr Finchley will announce the winning team and present the prizes when the gentlemen join us in a little while.'

'We are planning to perform a pantomime on Boxing Day; it is to be Cinderella. I do hope you are going to participate.'

Freddie scarcely managed to disguise her shudder of horror at the thought. 'I do not enjoy playacting, but would be happy to help with costumes or something of that sort.'

Lucy came across with several young ladies in tow. This group consisted of three erstwhile candidates and three debutantes. 'I am to play Cinderella, Freddie, but we have an ugly sister part available if you would like it?'

'You are too kind, but I shall politely decline your offer. How are you progressing with props and costumes?'

'Mrs Halston has provided us with two trunks of garments that will be ideal. I believe they were items belonging to her grandparents.'

One of the girls asked if there was to be dancing later. Freddie pointed to the four footmen staggering about with furniture at the far end of the drawing room. 'I believe so, otherwise why would the staff be clearing that end of the room? There was dancing the other night; who played the pianoforte?'

'My mama's companion, Mrs Evesham, volunteered, and she has said she is happy to do so tonight as well.' This welcome news came from another lady she had also forgotten the name of.

'Listen, I can hear movement from the dining room. Please excuse me; I am to assist with the presentation.' Freddie wasn't sure where the bolts of material and silver-topped walking canes had been put, and they would be needed when the names were announced. She enquired from one of the footmen who was now on his knees with the others preparing to roll up the handsome carpet.

'I think the things you are referring to, miss, are under that holland cover, behind the pillar over there.'

She thanked him and hurried over to check, and sure enough, these were the things that would be needed. The gentlemen strolled in, but neither Finchley nor his cousin were with them.

Had something untoward occurred to cause this delay? Freddie relaxed as they finally appeared, deep in conversation. Neither was smiling, but she thought she was the only one to have noticed this. Finchley beckoned to her and she hurried across.

'Is everything all right? Is it to do with that man?'

'It is, but nothing for you to worry

about. I shall tell you later. Unless you are desperate to join in with the dancing, why don't you come to my study, where we can talk in private after I've presented the prizes?'

'I will do so. How are you going to attract the attention of this noisy crowd? Perhaps you should get your butler to bang the gong.'

Instead he stepped into the space made by the missing furniture, and stood there for a few moments until those nearest were aware he was waiting to speak. Then he asked the assembled company for silence. Although he hadn't shouted, so commanding was his presence that there was instant quiet.

He announced the winners and handed out the prizes. The recipients were all delighted. Freddie waited for him to explain the second part of the prize but he did not do so. Presumably he had decided the gifts were sufficiently valuable and there was no necessity to add any more disturbance to the gathering.

She managed to slip away when the music started and waited in the hall for him to join her. She didn't like to be so presumptuous as to enter his study without him being with her.

* * *

Richard was seething. His careful plans to keep Lucy's name free of scandal were unravelling. Somehow word of what had happened had reached Rushton's parents, and they were not satisfied with the explanation. They were unbothered by the fact that their son was injured, but were determined to discover why he had been struck down. They had dismissed the false tale, that he had fallen and hit his head, immediately.

Richard's plans to propose must be put to one side until the matter was settled. His hesitation was not due to having his name associated with a possible scandal. When he asked his darling lady to marry him, he wanted her to accept his offer because she returned his regard and not because she had no other option.

His mouth curved when he saw she was waiting as far away from the kissing bough as she could. 'Come, Freddie; we must talk.'

She followed him in silence, immediately aware that all was not well. He could not think of any other young lady of his acquaintance who would be so sensitive to another's feelings. Once they were safely in his domain, he decided to tell her the whole.

'I didn't want to tell you this, as I don't wish you to feel in any way obliged to me because of my actions. I agreed to settle Rushton's debts and added a substantial extra amount so he can go abroad, to the colonies or India. And in turn, he agreed to say that he had fallen and hit his head on the mantelpiece.'

He had expected her to protest at his involvement, but instead she smiled. 'It is exactly what I would have expected you to do. You are a good man and I appreciate your help.' He was about to speak again when she held up her hand. 'However, I shall have to inform my father what took place, and he will reimburse you fully for your expenditure.'

'You will do no such thing, Freddie. This outrage took place under my roof and was perpetrated by a member of a family we consider to be our good friends. I must insist that you leave matters to me. If your father is involved, then things will escalate; and however hard we try, your sister's name will become blackened.'

Freddie bit her lip, closed her eyes for a second, and then nodded. 'Very well, I can see the logic in what you say. Why did you feel the need to tell me this? Surely it would have been better to keep it a secret?'

He quickly explained, and she sighed. 'I don't understand. Why would Rushton's parents not accept his story and be glad they would have no scandal attached to their name? If they talk to his cronies, Lucy's name is bound to be mentioned. Could they be hoping to force her into marrying him?'

'As they don't know she was involved, that cannot be the reason. I think instead that they have had enough nonsense from their son and wish to recompense whoever he has mistreated. The fact that it took place in an unoccupied bedchamber, and that they know their son to be a debaucher of young ladies, was enough to point them in the right direction.'

'Richard, what are we to do? How can we stop them before my sister's involvement becomes known?'

14

'We cannot remain closeted in here together any longer or there will be talk about us, as well as about my sister,' Freddie said firmly.

'I suggest that you return to the drawing room, and I shall speak to Rushton's father again. I noticed that neither his mother nor his sister were present at dinner. That cannot be a good sign.'

'I will circulate and see if anyone is talking about what happened. I didn't notice their absence, but I'm sure there were others who did so and must be curious.'

Richard strode off in the direction of the billiard room and Freddie headed for the hall. Hopefully, if she drifted around there for a while, no one would suspect she had been alone with Richard. His behaviour over the past day had caused her to change her opinion of him.

This did not mean, of course, that she would ever contemplate marriage to a gentleman so dictatorial. When she did decide to tie the knot, it would be with someone more accommodating, someone who would allow her continue doing the things she loved and not expect her to be a compliant wife.

There were several couples in the makeshift ballroom performing a lively country dance, and these were being watched by half a dozen others. The remainder of the party were either having a comfortable coze, or were sitting at a card table.

'There you are, Frederica. Are you not to dance tonight?'

'No, Mama; you know I do not enjoy it.'

This comment caused a ripple of disbelief around the circle of ladies in which her mother was sitting. Freddie smiled brightly. 'I shall, of course, dance at the ball.'

She smoothed the back of her gown and sat next to her mother on the padded settle. 'I cannot remember enjoying myself so much, despite the fact that I have had two accidents in as many days.'

No sooner had she said this than she wished the words back. Word of her falling on the ice had not reached any of these ladies. Her amusing rendition of this story was enough to satisfy the listeners, but she saw her mother eyeing her speculatively.

'Come, Frederica, I wish to watch your sister dancing. You will join me.'

She had no option but to comply, but did so reluctantly, knowing she was about to be quizzed on her relationship with Richard.

'Tell me at once, is there something going on between you and Mr Finchley? Although he is not titled, he is a member of the *ton* and would do very well for you. Although I own I am surprised he is looking in your direction. It is a great pity the earl is no longer considering taking a bride, as I had great hopes that he would settle on your sister.'

'Mama, I will not be coerced into a match I do not like. Mr Finchley believes that I might suit him, but he is quite wrong on that score.' Again, she regretted her intemperate words. She had revealed to her mother that he was interested in her, and now she would never hear the last of it.

'As he has yet to speak to your father, one must not make premature assumptions. However, my dear, if he does speak to your papa, he will give his permission and you will have no option but to accept the offer if it is made.'

'In the unlikely event that he does ask for my hand, then I will of course give it my full attention.'

She recalled the conversation she and her sister had had before they arrived, and wondered if it was too late to set in motion their scheme to give their host and his cousin a disgust of them both.

The dance came to an end, and Lucy

curtsied to her partner and hurried over to join them. 'Freddie, I believe I might have torn my hem. Would you come with me and inspect it?'

'Of course. Excuse us, Mama. We will be back directly.'

Freddie took her sister's arm and guided her out through the second exit that led directly to the dining room. Once they were safely inside, she closed the door. 'What is it, dearest? What has agitated you?'

'The gentleman I was dancing with mentioned that Mr Rushton and his family have left.'

'Surely that is not a bad thing? If they are gone, then there can be no further gossip.'

'He told me that Mr Rushton had been attacked by a member of this house party and the altercation had been over one of the young ladies present.' Lucy collapsed onto the nearest chair. 'It can only be a matter of time before the truth comes out, and then I shall be ruined. I don't know who the person

was who intended to find us in a compromising position — but whoever it is
must know it was I who Rushton intended
to seduce.'

'Mr Finchley is taking care of matters.
You can be very sure he will not allow
that to happen. He must have evicted
the family, because I cannot believe they
would have left of their own volition.
Come, Lucy. We cannot remain in here
any longer, for we will draw attention to
ourselves. The most important thing is
for both of us to continue as if nothing
untoward has happened and pray that
whatever measures have been taken by
our host will be successful.'

'I wish we had never come here. I
should have refused when Papa suggested it. Why cannot we leave as we
planned?'

'Because it will be Christmas tomorrow, and we cannot travel then. We must
brazen it out, and in the meantime, we
must try and persuade our parents to
return home as soon as may be.'

They returned to the drawing room

arm in arm, smiling and chatting as if they had not a care in the world. Freddie detected no surreptitious looks or sly glances from anyone, so thought they were safe from scandal for the moment.

★ ★ ★

Richard pounded up the staircase to the apartment the Rushtons were occupying. He would try there first, and if he was unsuccessful, he would investigate the chamber at the far end of the house where the young gentlemen were housed. He could hardly go in search of the sister — there had been more than enough food for gossip without adding to it.

He knocked loudly on the door and was pleased when Mr Rushton opened it himself. 'Come in, Finchley. I was expecting you.'

Richard saw at once that they were in the process of packing their belongings. 'There is no need for you to leave so hastily, sir. The weather is appalling, and I would not be sanguine about you travelling at night in such conditions.'

'We live less than an hour's drive from here. I'm certain we can complete that distance without mishap, even in the dark. My son is a disgrace, and as soon as he has recovered from his injury, he will be packed off to work for the East India Company. He will not return until he has mended his ways.'

'It might well be the making of him, sir.'

'He insists that his injury was self-inflicted, but I know him too well to think it is the truth.' He held up his hand to stop Richard from speaking. 'I've no wish to know the truth; whoever he attempted to harm has suffered enough.' He reached into his waistcoat pocket and held out the letter of credit Richard had made out to his son.

'I thank you for your generosity, but I will not have him rewarded for his perfidy.' He tore the paper into pieces and tossed it into the fire. 'I can only apologise again for the distress and trouble that wretched boy has caused. I can assure you that no word of this will ever be spoken by my family. However, I suggest that you speak to Tewkesbury's son — they are thick as thieves, and if my son was up to no good, then young Tewkesbury will have been in the middle of it too.'

There was no more to be said. 'I shall do that immediately.' He bowed, and Rushton returned the gesture. Presumably his wife and daughter were busy with their packing in their own chambers.

Richard had no idea which of the youngsters was Tewkesbury's son, so he would have to find his cousin and get him to point him out.

Abingdon was skipping about the place, partnering a hopeful young lady in a country dance. He was surprised to see that both Freddie and her sister were also in the set. His beloved did not appear to be enjoying the experience.

He positioned himself a safe distance from the fray so he would not be obliged to ask anyone to dance, and then watched her promenade and curtsy with an older gentleman. She moved with grace, and he doubted anyone else would be aware of what he could see at once — that dancing was not her forte.

Somehow he had to prevent his cousin from dancing again, and decided he would just have to march over and grab him by the arm and to hell with those who thought his behaviour odd. He could do as he damn well pleased in his own home.

The music stopped and he closed the distance between himself and his cousin so speedily that he was beside him before he had time to interact with another young lady.

'Tewkesbury's son — which one is he?'

Abingdon looked around. 'He's not on the dance floor. He is wearing a red and gold striped waistcoat, so will be easy to find. Do you require my assistance?'

'No, I can deal with this myself. The Rushtons are leaving tonight. I need to ensure young Tewkesbury doesn't mention Lucy's name when he hears his friend has gone.'

Richard realised he should have asked the height and hair colour of his quarry, as gentlemen with their backs turned did not reveal the colour of their waistcoats. The person he sought was not amongst the gentlemen in the drawing room playing cards, so the most likely place to find him was the billiard room.

The passageway that led there was decidedly chill, as there were no fireplaces along this wall — also the fact that there were windows which were unshuttered did not help the situation. He snapped his fingers at a lurking footman.

'Get the shutters closed. It should have been done hours ago.' Then something occurred to him — the person to ask about the whereabouts of young Tewkesbury was a servant. 'Is Mr

Tewkesbury in the billiards room?'

'He is, sir. He went past but a moment ago.'

Richard left the man frantically closing shutters and continued on his way. He had not come up with a plan for removing this gentleman from the company of his cronies, but hoped inspiration would strike when he arrived.

The room was occupied by only four people. Three of them seemed engrossed in a game, but the fourth was staring morosely into the fire.

'Mr Tewkesbury, a moment of your time.'

The young man jerked forwards, and was only saved from stepping into the fire by Richard's quick thinking.

'I beg your pardon. I did not mean to startle you.'

'I was expecting you to come in search of me, Mr Finchley. Shall we go somewhere more private to converse?'

'My study would be best. I've an excellent brandy waiting to be drunk.'

The thought of a stiff drink seemed

to cheer the unfortunate fellow somewhat, as he almost smiled. After a brisk walk through the house, they reached their destination, and Richard pushed open the door to allow Tewkesbury to enter first. He left the young man to find himself a seat whilst he poured two generous measures of brandy. When he turned, his guest was still hovering in the centre of the room.

'Sit down. Here you are; drink this before we talk. You look as though you need it more than I.'

The alcohol vanished in two gulps, and Richard brought the decanter over and refilled it. He settled himself opposite. 'You obviously know why I wish to talk to you. Let us not prevaricate. Rushton and his family have left — do I have to insist that you do the same?'

'I should never have agreed to help him. I owed him a favour; he got me out of a scrape or two when we were at Oxford together.' He hesitated and seemed reluctant to continue. Richard waited, not wishing to interrupt.

'I thought it an elaborate game of hide and go seek, and only understood his true intentions after I heard he had been injured. I can assure you, sir, I shall never speak of what transpired, and do not know the name of the young lady he was attempting to trap into marriage.'

'In which case, the matter is closed. You are well rid of him — he is being sent to India for a few years, so you will not be bothered by him again.'

'I shall not be the only one delighted with that news. Are you quite sure you don't wish me to leave?'

'I do not. Finish your drink and return to the drawing room.'

This brandy also vanished in two swallows, and Tewkesbury was on his feet and out of the door as if his coat-tails were on fire. Richard was tempted to refill his own glass but decided against it. He wished to keep a clear head, as he was now in a position to pursue his original objective — that of convincing the volatile young lady he had come to love that she should marry him.

So surprised was he that he was in love that his hand clenched on the glass and it shattered beneath his fingers. Fortunately, he was still wearing his evening gloves, or the damage would have been far worse. Even so, the white material was now stained red. He carefully picked the shards of glass from his palm and then eased the glove from his injured hand.

This was ideal to use as a cloth to clean the damaged area. He smiled ruefully as he inspected the two small gashes which, despite his best efforts, were oozing blood. He strode across to the bell-strap and pulled it. He needed the housekeeper's attention. The poor woman must think the world had gone mad, as she had been called upon more in the past two days than she had in the past ten years.

She was efficiency itself. 'The cuts are deep but don't need stitches, sir. A bandage will suffice. If you keep your gloves on, no one will be aware that you have hurt your hand.'

His valet brought down the required objects, and he was fully restored in less time than it would take to dance a minuet. He would ask the pianist if she could play the music for a waltz. It would be an ideal dance to woo Freddie.

On his return to join the company, his head was still spinning from the extraordinary knowledge that the impossible had taken place. Marriage had never been a priority for him; he had always supposed that one day he would enter the parson's mousetrap and set up his nursery with a young lady from the top echelons of society. He had expected his choice would be a beautiful but quiet and obedient lady. Someone who would not cause any disruption to his well-ordered life and would happily settle in to Finchley Hall along with his other female relatives.

What he hadn't anticipated was that he would fall neck over crop for a most unsuitable woman. Not only was she not from an aristocratic family, but she was also the opposite of what he had thought he wanted in a wife. Being married to Freddie would never be dull, that was for sure. She reminded him of a flighty mare he owned, one he had only got to accept the bit and saddle by approaching the process in a different way. First, he had won the animal's trust, then her affection, and only after that had he attempted to ride her.

He would put aside his desire to declare to the company that he had found his future bride until he was sure she returned his regard in some measure. He thought it highly unlikely that she had already fallen in love with him, but that could come later. They had the rest of their lives to spend together; if she didn't love him now, he would change her mind once they were sharing the marital bed.

He was a practical man, not given to romantic fancies, and marrying a woman who did not reciprocate his feelings was not a deterrent to the union. Respect and affection were sufficient, in his opinion, for a successful marriage, and he was certain Freddie felt both of those for him.

He pushed his whimsical thoughts aside as he entered the drawing room. He saw Freddie talking to her sister whilst two of his female cousins discussed with the pianist what tune to play next. He strolled in that direction and arrived in time to intervene.

'Madam, do you know a tune suitable for the waltz?'

'I do, Mr Finchley; in fact, I know several. I hadn't liked to play them, as I wasn't sure the countess and Mrs Finchley would approve.'

'This is a private party, so we may do as we please.' Richard winked at his cousins and they giggled. First mission accomplished; now all he had to do was convince Freddie to dance with him, and to do so before any of the circling bucks could get in first.

'Miss Halston, there is to be a waltz.

Would you care to dance it with me?'
He pitched his voice so that anyone
within a few yards must have heard
him. This meant she could not refuse
without looking impolite.

15

'Thank you, sir. I should be delighted to stand up with you. However, I must warn you that I am not proficient in this modern dance, and you might well regret your decision.'

He nodded solemnly. 'I'm sure that I shall not.' He offered his arm and she took it, knowing she was the centre of attention. Her mother would be the one watching most keenly.

For a horrible few moments, they were the only ones on the cleared space that served as the dance floor tonight, but then other couples drifted on to join them. The music started, and whatever Freddie had been going to say was forgotten as Richard swept her away in time to the music.

He was an expert dancer, and within the first few seconds she relaxed and allowed herself to be guided around the floor. She had not been lying when she said she was an indifferent dancer herself, but tonight everything was different.

'It is customary, sweetheart, to converse with one's partner and not stare at the floor.'

She raised her head and returned his smile. 'I was anticipating a disaster, but it would appear I am in safe hands. In fact, I own I am enjoying the experience.'

'I'm delighted to hear you say so. I'm certain we are the handsomest couple in the room. I — '

Rudely, she interrupted him. 'Why didn't you allow the winning team to rule over us for the next few days? I was quite disappointed at the omission.'

He spun her around the end of the room, almost lifting her from her feet, and she was too busy trying to remain upright to worry about his lack of response. Eventually she caught her breath enough to speak, but seeing the glint in his eye, she wisely refrained. It would be better to wait until they were stationary before she pulled the tiger's tail a second time.

She curtsied and he bowed, but instead of escorting her back to join her sister, he whisked her through the side entrance and down the passageway towards the hall.

'Enough of this, sir. I will not be dragged about the place like one of your hounds.' She tried to detach her hand from his arm but he trapped it against his side.

'If you attempt to stop, my love, I shall carry you. I'm determined to speak to you in private.'

She stopped struggling. 'I suppose that being led is better than being carried like a parcel. If you are intending to propose to me, you will be wasting your breath. I have not changed my mind on that subject.'

She had expected him to be in high dudgeon at her outrageous statement, but he laughed. 'I've no intention of proposing to you. I merely wish to kiss you under the mistletoe.'

This was the outside of enough. If he didn't wish to marry her, then he shouldn't take liberties with her person. If she screamed, would he be so horrified he would let her go? Would the resulting unpleasantness that would engulf them both be worth it?

Then she decided to approach the matter from the opposite direction. Instead of lagging behind him, she increased her pace. 'Why did you not say so? I am more than delighted to kiss you, as long as you don't expect me to marry you afterwards.'

She thought he would pause and reconsider, shocked by her boldness; but instead he released her hand, put his arm around her waist, and all but ran the last few yards.

There was little point in being coy when she had positively encouraged his disgraceful behaviour. She threaded her arms around his neck and tilted her head to allow him access to her lips. His arm drew her closer so that every inch of her was pressed against his hard frame. Then, with the other hand, he cupped the back of her head and lowered his own so his mouth was touching hers.

What happened next was so unexpected, so exciting, that Freddie quite forgot she had decided she didn't wish to marry him. A young lady did not passionately embrace a gentleman in the way that she was doing if she wasn't already betrothed to him.

She was quite breathless when he eventually raised his head. 'I think that will do, my love. We have attracted more than enough attention, don't you think?'

Freddie rested her head against his shoulder, not daring to look round and see who might have watched her disgraceful display. The kissing bough hanging so temptingly beneath the crystal chandelier was for the exchange of a chaste kiss only — not what had just taken place between them.

Her lips were tingling. In fact, everywhere was tingling. 'Who is watching us?'

'My mother and your mother — do you need to know the names of anyone else?'

'I have fallen into your trap most neatly, have I not?' If she was going to marry him, then he would have to suffer some discomfort first. 'I hope you intend to go down on one knee and make me a formal offer, Richard. I shall be satisfied with nothing less.'

His expression changed from wary to something she didn't recognise. He didn't hesitate, but dropped to one knee, still holding her hand.

'Darling Freddie, will you do me the inestimable honour of becoming my wife? Make me the happiest of men.'

'Thank you for your offer, Richard. I accept. Although I cannot say I am delighted at the prospect, I am resigned, which will have to be enough for you.'

If she had expected him to be dismayed by her less than enthusiastic response, she was disappointed. He rose to his feet and embraced her as thoroughly a second time as he had the first.

'Finchley, that is quite enough. Might I be the first to congratulate you on your betrothal?' Her future mother-in-law had glided silently across the hall and was standing rigid with disapproval beside them.

'You may indeed, Mama. As you can see, it was a *coup de foudre*. I had never expected to fall in love so swiftly — if I'm honest I had not expected to fall in love at all — but here we are.' He raised Freddie's hand and kissed the knuckles. 'Forgive me, my love. I must go and speak to your father immediately. I believe I should have done that before I spoke to you.'

He strode off, leaving her to face the accusatory faces of those gathered around her. Well, her mother wasn't one of them; she was looking in high alt at having achieved so successful a marriage for her eldest daughter. Mrs Finchley was staring at her in a most disconcerting way, as were the other ladies who had come to watch what they had hoped would be a disaster. Instead, they had witnessed a triumph.

This woman was to be her mother-in-law, and she would probably have to share this house with her for the foreseeable future. Therefore, it was better they were on speaking terms. She curtsied politely. 'I apologise if our behaviour has shocked you, madam, but Richard and I knew we were destined to be together the moment we set eyes on each other. If he is satisfied that I am the bride for him, then I hope you will accept his choice.'

'I must disagree with you, Miss Halston. My son told me you were the last person he would ever consider marrying.' She moved closer so her words could not be overheard. 'You will learn soon enough that desire is not the same as love. When the honeymoon period is over, my son will realise his error and regret his decision. If you do not wish to have a miserable life, I suggest that you tell him you have changed your mind so he may marry someone more suitable.'

Richard found Halston blowing a cloud on the terrace despite the fact that it was snowing. 'I have come to ask your permission to marry Freddie, sir. I apologise that I did not speak to you before I made my offer.'

'Did she accept you?'

'She did — and she did it in full view of half a dozen of my guests.'

'Then the matter is settled. Although I came here determined to secure the earl for one of my girls, I have changed my opinion on the matter. It was a foolhardy scheme, and I would never wish to force either of my daughters to marry someone they did not wish to.'

'I love her, sir. I would not have offered for her hand otherwise. At the moment she has not admitted she feels the same, but I'm confident she will soon realise that she would never have agreed to become engaged otherwise.'

'To tell you the truth, my boy, my Freddie is not like other young ladies.

She spends her time painting in her studio or in the kennels or stables. She has never enjoyed the things that my Lucy does. You must not marry her if you are not prepared to allow her the freedom to do as she wishes.'

'I shall be quite happy for her to continue with those interests, but when we are married, she will be answerable to me and I shall expect her to run my house, bring up my children, and act as my hostess. These responsibilities must come first.'

'I expect I have been an overindulgent father, and it will be no bad thing for her to comport herself correctly for a change. When do you intend to get married? Is it to be a long engagement?'

'I thought in the spring. It will give us time to get to know each other better and for me to refurbish the house to her taste.'

'Splendid, splendid. Does Mrs Halston know the good news?'

'She was there when I proposed, sir, and has no doubt spread the word throughout the company, so there will be no need for a formal announcement.'

'As you say, as you say. I shall have my man of business attend you in the new year to organise the financial matters.'

'I am aware that your daughter has a substantial dowry, Halston, but I have no need of it. I — '

'If you don't have need of it, then you must see that it remains available to her. I must go in; my wife will wish to discuss the wedding plans. My daughter will be married in our church; we shall hold the wedding breakfast at our house. I hope that is satisfactory.'

Halston obviously didn't give a damn if Richard agreed or not. The man stalked off, disapproval evident in every stride. Richard regretted his impolite comment that inferred that his future mother-in-law was a gossip.

All Finchley and Abingdon marriages took place in their own church, and Richard was determined that his would not be different. He might not agree with the wedding venue, but he certainly thought that Freddie's trust fund should remain in her name. Then he reconsidered — if he had access to her fortune, then he could give more to his cousin and ensure that not only was Abingdon Manor restored, but Abingdon would have sufficient in his coffers to marry where he chose and not be obliged to pick an heiress.

It was fortunate indeed that Lord Rushton had torn up his letter of credit. He was about to go in search of his future wife when something occurred to him that gave him pause. When this scheme to attract an heiress in return for a title had been mooted, he had not been in favour. Yet here he was, about to be married to one of the candidates and intending to use her fortune in exactly the same way that his cousin would have done.

This realisation left a nasty taste in his mouth. Was he marrying Freddie because he loved her, or were the reasons more complex? He found her desirable and could not wait to make love to her — he had thoroughly compromised her, so in the end would have had no option but to offer to marry her — and by this marriage would be able to put right the depredations caused by his grandfather to the family home. As he had no notion exactly what the term 'love' actually meant, he could not be sure he was experiencing such a feeling.

This was hardly a subject he would care to discuss with his parent, and as far as he knew, his cousin claimed he had been in love at least half a dozen times since he had reached his majority. Richard decided he would continue this investigation at a later date — perhaps there was a volume in the library that would clarify the matter for him.

Now he must concentrate on behaving in a way that would be expected from a gentleman in love with his betrothed. He grimaced when he remembered how he had observed other gentlemen so afflicted by this emotion that they penned nauseating poetry to their loved one, followed the young lady around with a fatuous expression, and took every opportunity available to praise their future bride in the most fulsome manner possible.

He would do none of these things. However, he could demonstrate to Freddie by his actions how he felt. He cared not what others thought, as long as she believed that he loved her.

★ ★ ★

Freddie stared at the woman for a moment, unable to comprehend what she had said. It would have been sensible to curtsy politely and walk away, but she was not famous for doing the sensible thing.

'Madam, I'm so glad that you have made your opinion on the matter so plain. It gives me permission to be equally direct. You will have vacated these premises by the time I move in.

Do I make myself clear?'

Mrs Finchley did not retract; did not apologise and try to make amends for her comments. Her eyes were like flint and her lips narrowed. 'Is it your wish to evict the countess and her daughters as well? I can assure you, Miss Halston, that in the unlikely event that you do in fact marry my son, you will have to do so in the knowledge that he always puts family first. I have been chatelaine here since my arrival, and intend to remain so until I depart.'

'That is exactly what I said. I'm so glad that you agree with me. I have no objection to Richard's aunt and cousins remaining here until Abingdon Manor has been renovated.' Freddie nodded and walked away with her head held high. She had been well aware that the wretched woman had been talking about her death when she had talked about departure, but it had fallen neatly into her hands.

Freddie was too angry to rejoin the party, but had no wish to retire. She would go to the stables and see Othello and the dogs, but first she must remove her evening gown, as she had no wish to spoil it.

On the way there, she used the less prestigious staircase and met nobody. Now warmly dressed in her oldest gown, stout boots and thick cloak, she was ready to brave the elements. The side door was, as last time, unlocked. She pulled it back and was almost lifted from her feet by a blast of icy wind liberally laced with snow.

Perhaps it would be unwise to go out in such weather, even for so short a distance; but once she had made up her mind about a thing, she always saw it through. Another reason for making herself scarce was that Richard would not be pleased with her when he heard what she had said to his mama.

There had been ample time for her to consider what had been spoken on both sides, and although Mrs Finchley should not have said what she did, it did not mean that Freddie's response was in any way acceptable. It was not her place to tell anyone living in this house that they must leave. Even when she was Mrs Finchley herself, she would have to accept whatever decision her husband made, whether she liked it or not.

The hounds found her before she reached the stable yard, and she was grateful for their company. 'Take me to Othello, boys. I doubt I could find my way in this blizzard.'

The cobbles underfoot were slippery, and only by hanging onto the scruffs of the dogs was Freddie able to maintain her balance. The dozen or so loose boxes were firmly shut against the elements, but she knew where the stallion was located.

At this time of night, the stable hands and outside men would be safely in their own abodes. There was little likelihood of her meeting one of them on this foolhardy excursion. One would have thought she might have learned her lesson after venturing out in bad weather when she and Lucy had tried to escape a few nights ago. Yet here she was once more, behaving in an unseemly manner, and she did not care one jot.

It would have been sensible to open both parts of the door, but the wind was so strong she feared they would bang against the wall and alert someone to her presence. Instead, she undid the top half and toppled head first over it into the stable. Smoke and Wolf followed, and she was able to grab hold of the swinging door before it clattered backwards.

The occupant of the box, despite his reputation for being savage, welcomed all three of them with whickers and snuffles of delight.

'I am pleased to see you too, old fellow. But please allow me to straighten my garments before you knock me off my feet.'

The horse didn't budge until she put one palm on his neck and the other on his chest and gently pressed. He backed up until she had room to move. The dogs flopped onto the straw, but she was unwilling to join them in case she sat on something unpleasant. It was impossible to see what was underfoot in the inky blackness.

'I cannot stay out here all night with you, however much I might wish to. But I shall tell you one thing. I have made the most dreadful error of judgement in allowing my passion to rule my head. I cannot possibly be in love with your master after so short a time, and it would be the height of foolishness to marry him.'

16

Richard went in search of Freddie, but was unable to locate her, and was resigned to the fact that she had retired. He could hardly follow her to her apartment, although he was tempted to do so. He had had enough of gaiety for one night and retreated to his study, closing the door firmly behind him.

He pulled back a shutter and peered into the darkness. It was snowing heavily, so there would be no possibility of walking to the church for matins. Foster had already informed him that the curate was safely installed somewhere in the house and that the service would be held in the ballroom at ten o'clock.

He had left instructions that the tea tray be brought in early so that everyone would have retired before midnight. His guests had been informed that they would be expected to attend the service and that no breakfast would be served, but a substantial luncheon would be available in the main dining room at midday.

There was plenty of correspondence and estate business to occupy him until the house was quiet. It would now be safe to emerge from his temporary isolation and make his own way to bed. He glanced at the long-case clock ticking loudly in the corner, and saw it would be Christmas Day in a quarter of an hour.

He extinguished the candles, checked the fire was safely banked, and stepped into the corridor. Even at this distance from the grand hall, the sweet smells of applewood and cinnamon filled his nostrils. The house was appreciably warmer with the yule log burning there, and he decided he would keep this fire going until the winter was over.

As Richard approached, there was an icy blast which flickered the candles burning in the wall sconces. The chandelier had been extinguished, and this vast space was filled with shadows. If he had been a superstitious man, he might have thought he was in the presence of a Christmas ghost.

The draught had come from someone either exiting or entering through the side door — he headed that way and was unsurprised to meet Freddie, as he had already guessed who it might be.

'Good evening, sweetheart. Have you been visiting my stallion?' Then he saw she had come in accompanied by his dogs. He was about to snap his fingers and send them out but reconsidered.

'I have, but that is not all I was doing. One of the horses in the barn showed signs of colic, and I have spent the past few hours walking him up and down. He is fully recovered now, so there's no need for you to go out.'

There was little point in remonstrating, in telling her she should have sent word to him and allowed his competent head groom to deal with the matter. Freddie would do as she pleased, whatever anyone said to the contrary.

He reached across her and slipped the bolts into the hasps. The only reason the door had been left unlocked was because someone had been aware she was outside. He would make enquiries tomorrow, as he was curious to know which of his staff she had bewitched.

'I'm glad that you are still up, as there is something I need to say to you.' She looked directly at him and he didn't need her to continue.

'You wish to reconsider our betrothal?'

'I do. Before I continue, have you spoken to your mother recently?'

'I have not. She will not approve of our engagement, as she considers I would be marrying beneath me.'

'That is exactly what she said. She also said that you are marrying me out of lust not love, and that we will both regret it. I think she is right. We have only known each other a few days, and most of that time we have been at daggers drawn.' She paused as if unsure if she should tell him the rest.

'I have been thinking the same thing. Unfortunately, my dear, we were seen by several people, and we have no choice but to marry, unless both our reputations are to be destroyed.'

'You do not know the whole of it. I told Mrs Finchley she would have to leave here when we were married, as I would not share a house with her.'

'Good grief! I doubt that that was well received. What about my aunt and cousins? Do you wish me to evict them as well?' He was trying hard to hide his smile. He could think of no one else of his acquaintance who would have dared to stand up to his formidable parent, and he admired her for it.

'No; I said I was willing for them to stay until the earl has restored his home and they can return there.'

* * *

This was not going at all how Freddie had expected. Richard was not enraged at her impertinence, but struggling to contain his amusement. 'As we have decided not to marry, then . . . '

'We have decided no such thing, sweetheart. I believe all we have clarified is the fact that we are not in love but find each other desirable.'

A scalding heat spread from her toes to her crown at his plain speaking. 'That is a most improper thing to say. And even if it was true, it is hardly sufficient upon which to base a lifelong partnership.'

'I should say that we have more than most couples in our favour. Do you like me?'

She was somewhat disconcerted by his question and was tempted to answer in the negative. 'I did not when I first met you, but you seem to have changed. I thought you proud and disdainful.'

'And now?'

'And now I think you are annoying, dictatorial and . . . and kind, intelligent and good company.'

'I thought you beneath my touch and

prejudiced against the *ton*, but I too have come to a different conclusion. You are impertinent and outrageous but also intelligent, witty and generous.'

She realised that she had not answered his original question. 'I do not wish to like you, as you are everything that I disapprove of, but I find that I do. Do you feel the same?'

'I consider you a friend, and I do not have many of them. As we do not have a choice in this matter, sweetheart . . . '

'Of course we do. I shall break off the engagement, and I'm sure that society will heave a collective sigh of relief that someone of my ilk will not be joining them.'

'I don't think you fully understand, Freddie. It is not just you who will be ostracised, but your family too. I will be labelled a rake, and you . . . I think it better not to say out loud what will be said about your behaviour.'

She was about to disagree, but finally understood that what he said was the truth. They were trapped into this arrangement and must make the best of it. 'What about your mother?'

'I can assure you, my love, that I shall insist that she move to the Dower House. If that is not to her taste, then she can occupy one of my smaller estates instead.'

'I shall make you an impossible wife. I am used to going my own way.'

He moved so swiftly she had no time to step away. He gathered her close, slipping his arms beneath her cloak, and she could not stop herself from leaning into the embrace. 'You will find, darling girl, that being my wife has more advantages than not.'

His kiss was brief, his lips hard, and she wished it had carried on for longer. Unless you were a lady of the night, such pleasures as this could only be shared with one's husband.

'Very well. If you insist, then I shall agree to marry you.'

'The matter was never in any doubt, my love. However, I should much prefer to make love to you when you do not smell so strongly of the stable.'

He was holding her at arm's length now, and she laughed at his expression of distaste. 'Then I fear, Richard, that you are going to be disappointed. You will discover that I prefer to spend my time outside with both horses and dogs, and I am not intending to change my ways.'

'That is another thing we must discuss, but not now. I think it high time we retired. Do not forget that the service to celebrate our Lord's birthday will take place at ten in the ballroom.' She was unceremoniously bundled onto the staircase and sent on her way with a sharp slap on her posterior. His laughter followed her as she scampered up the stairs.

Freddie tossed her soiled garments into a heap in the corner of the dressing room, and then draped her cloak over a chair in front of the fire so it would be dry in the morning. She quickly washed herself from head to toe before pulling her nightdress on. As she was drifting off to sleep, she heard the distant sound of church bells celebrating Christmas Day. She had much to be thankful for today. She had somehow become betrothed to a most attractive gentleman, one who made her pulse race whenever she saw him. The fact that he was also as rich as Croesus was in his favour, as she could be certain he wasn't marrying her for her money.

Smoke and Wolf had flopped down at the end of her bed, and she rather liked the idea that they were there — although the pungent aroma coming from them as their wet coats dried made her regret her decision to bring them upstairs.

She was woken the next morning by an ear-splitting scream and the crash of crockery.

'Mercy me! Whatever next! What are those horrible dogs doing in here?' Mary screeched.

Both dogs were on their feet and cowering in the corner. Freddie threw back the covers and snatched up her cloak. 'I am so sorry. I intended to take them down before you came in, but have overslept.' Her maid was weeping. She was not fond of canines at the best of times. The sooner Wolf and Smoke were gone, the better.

'Hush now. You are frightening them with your noise. See — they are desperate to get away from you.'

Mary paused in her wailing and looked at the hounds, who were shivering and whining; they looked piteously back at her. Freddie doubted they would ask to come up here again, which was probably a good thing in the circumstances.

'I'm going to run down and let them out whilst you clear up this mess.' There was no time to find footwear, and Freddie sincerely hoped that if she was unfortunate enough to meet anybody apart from a member of staff, the enveloping folds of her cloak would disguise the fact that she was improperly dressed and had bare feet.

She was halfway down the stairs when she was met by the young footman who had kindly left the door unbolted for her. 'I'll take them, miss. The master is already downstairs.'

'Thank you.'

As she rushed into her bedchamber, she remembered it was the Lord's birthday and there would be no breakfast until after the service in the ballroom. Mary was still on her knees, collecting shards of broken crockery.

'Leave that for the chambermaid, Mary, and please go down and fetch me something else to eat.'

With a sniff of disapproval, her maid stalked off. Whilst she was gone, Freddie picked up the remaining bits and found some old rags to mop up the spilt chocolate. She had not discarded her cloak, as the room was cold — the fire had not burned bright enough to remove the overnight chill.

*   *   *

Richard had been unable to sleep, so was up earlier than was usual. He checked that the ballroom had been set out as instructed and that the lectern had been placed in front of the rows of chairs ready for the curate to lead the service.

The ballroom had been draped with garlands, ribbons and extra candles, and he wasn't sure this was correct for such a solemn occasion. Then he reconsidered. After all, today was a celebration of the arrival of Christ in this world, and the ballroom certainly looked celebratory.

His hounds should be outside for their morning constitutional — the kennelman would have their feed ready and must be wondering where they were. The side door was still bolted. Richard was about to ascend the stairs when the animals bounded down and greeted him enthusiastically.

'Good boys. I shall let you out myself.'

Then a footman appeared and bowed. 'I'll see to the dogs, sir.'

This must be the young man who had been helping Freddie. Richard vaguely recognised the man, but had no idea what his name was. He employed dozens of male servants, and as they were all dressed in a similar fashion, it was difficult to distinguish one from another.

'Your name?'

'Tom Hudson, sir.'

'Well, Tom Hudson, I am pleased that you have been assisting the future Mrs Finchley. You will be well recompensed in your box tomorrow.'

He strode up the stairs, determined to wish his future wife a merry Christmas. He tapped on the sitting room door, and on receiving no reply, he walked in. He could hear someone moving about in the bedchamber and pushed open the door.

'Devil take it! What do you think you're doing?' Freddie was on her knees cleaning up the remains of her morning chocolate and sweet rolls.

'I would think it quite obvious what I'm doing, so I assume that is a rhetorical question.'

'Leave it, please. You will do yourself

no favours with the staff.'

She sat back on her heels. 'My maid dropped the tray because I forgot your dogs were in here with me. It's hardly fair that she should have to clean up the mess when it was entirely my fault. She is frightened of dogs, and I should have remembered that and warned her.'

Ignoring her protest, Richard took hold of her elbows and lifted her from the floor. 'It is not her place to have an opinion on such matters.' He bundled her into the sitting room and pushed her gently onto the chaise longue. Only then did he notice she was not dressed beneath her cloak and her feet were bare.

'Stay where you are, sweetheart. I'll get the fire going again. You really should not wander about the place in disarray, especially as it is Christmas Day today.' Her smile disarmed him, and his annoyance at her hoydenish behaviour vanished.

'I am well aware of that, but your dogs needed to be let out, and that was more important than spending half an hour getting dressed. There might well have been a far worse mess to clear up if I had not taken them down immediately.'

After several vigorous kicks, the fire came to life. Richard threw a few logs and some coal onto it, and then found the blanket and put it over Freddie's legs. 'When we are married, I will not have the dogs upstairs with us. Whatever you might think, they are outdoor animals and much prefer to sleep in the kennels.'

'How is it that they are always roaming about loose if that is the case?'

'Unlike my other dogs, these two are pets, and therefore come and go as they please and are not confined.'

She smiled and gestured that he take a seat beside her. 'I seem to be having one accident after another since I've been here. You might not believe it, but I cannot recall the last time anything similar happened to me or because of me.'

'Are you blaming me for these

incidents, sweetheart?'

To his surprise, she reached out and took his hand. This was the first time she had initiated any contact between them.

'My answer is contradictory. If you were not here, I would not be having accidents; but you are not directly to blame. For some reason, I have found myself behaving quite out of character since I got here.' She smiled and his fingers tightened involuntarily on hers. 'I think it might be because I am drawn to you — I have never been so affected by a gentleman before, and it is quite disconcerting.'

'I too have found that I have changed since we met. I sincerely hope you think it is for the better.'

He leaned towards her, and she reciprocated. Then she released his hand and sat back as her maid came in with the tray.

'I shall leave you, sweetheart, to get ready. I shall call for you at a quarter to the hour.'

'I shall be ready in good time.'

Freddie's maid flinched as he walked past, and he regretted that the girl found him frightening. He must soften his attitude to her, as he would be seeing her more often than any other member of staff apart from his own valet, once he was married to her mistress.

★　★　★

Freddie devoured the items on the tray, glad that her healthy appetite had now returned in full. How could so much have changed in only five days? More had happened to her and Lucy since they arrived here than had happened in the past year — indeed, in the past five years.

Now she was engaged to be married to a gentleman she had only known since she had arrived at his house. Admittedly, they had spent more time together than most couples did in their entire engagement, but it was still too short a space of time to be taking such a drastic step.

Her first impression of her future husband had been that he was an arrogant, self-centred gentleman who considered himself superior to anyone not in his rarefied circle. She was quite certain he had felt equally strongly about her — he had thought her wild, impertinent and beneath his touch. Yet here they were, planning to be married. She should be in tatters at the prospect of spending her life with exactly the sort of person she most despised. In her opinion, members of the *ton* had no thought for anyone but themselves, and spent as much money in one afternoon at a gaming table or a millinery as one of their employees would earn in a lifetime.

However, the only member of this group she had met since she had arrived at Finchley Hall who had fulfilled her expectations was Richard's mother. Everyone else had been unfailingly polite, sociable and charming

— at least they had been once the treasure hunt had mixed the younger members of the party together. Freddie now believed the stiffness between the two sides had been caused by them being strangers rather than them being from different tiers of society.

Her prejudice and Richard's pride had caused them to clash initially, but now things were different between them. They had not discussed when they were to be married, and this was something that needed to be decided as soon as could be. Indeed, Freddie had yet to speak to her parents or her beloved sister about her unexpected engagement.

Lucy came in looking even more beautiful than usual. "That blue velvet is perfect on you, my love.' Freddie told her. 'It exactly matches the colour of your eyes.'

Her sister ignored this compliment. 'Am I to believe my ears? Are you now to be married to Mr Finchley? Why is it I am the last to hear?'

Freddie explained how the sudden

engagement had taken place. 'So you see, I have not even spoken to our parents about it. I can still hardly credit that after all we said before we came here, it is I who is to be married after all.'

'As long as you do not intend to marry until the spring, you have plenty of time to change your mind. I cannot believe you will be living so far away from home, and with a gentleman you scarcely know.'

'I am having difficulty adjusting to my new situation as well. For some inexplicable reason, we are drawn to each other. We are not in love; we are both quite clear on that subject. He is a very handsome gentleman, however, and I am lucky to have attracted his attention.'

'He is the lucky one. He would be bored within a month if he married any of the insipid young ladies who would be considered a more suitable choice for him. You are exactly what he needs; but I am not so sure he will be good for you.'

17

Richard was happy to escort his future bride and sister-in-law to the ballroom. His stomach rumbled loudly and both ladies giggled. 'I beg your pardon,' he said. 'Unlike you, I have eaten nothing since dinner last night.'

'Then let us hope, Mr Finchley, that you do not disturb the service with your gurgling,' Lucy said when she had stopped laughing.

'Why don't you steal something from the dining room?' Freddie suggested. 'I'm sure there will already be something edible in there.'

As Richard's stomach growled again, he thought he had better take Freddie's advice. 'Go ahead; I shall join you in a moment.'

The ballroom was on the opposite side of the house to the dining room, breakfast room and drawing room. He nodded and smiled at the people he passed going in the opposite direction, and hoped he could complete his mission and still be back before Christmas matins began. He strode into the dining room and pounced on a slice of game pie. He thought this would be enough to stop his insides complaining so loudly.

The sound of music echoed from the ballroom as he approached along with a dozen or more others. He could hear people behind him, so he wasn't late. Freddie was sitting in the front row and had left a space for him between herself and her sister. Fortunately, there was still a hum of conversation, and his progress was not unduly noted. He took the seat and Freddie smiled.

'Are we to have a turkey tonight, or maybe a swan or two?' Freddie asked him.

'It's usually turkey, but I'm sure next year you can insist that we risk the wrath of the king by stealing one of his birds for our Christmas dinner.'

The cleric shuffled from the side to

take his place at the lectern, and the room eventually fell silent. Whoever was playing the piano was not paying attention, and the music continued for at least another minute, causing sniggers and muffled laughter.

Richard had insisted there would be no hymns, carols or a sermon, and he rather regretted his decision now, as he would have liked to have heard Freddie sing. They stood up and sat down when required, recited psalms, made responses and then received the blessing.

His mother, aunt and cousins were sitting together on the other side of the aisle also on the front row. It was going to be interesting seeing how the two women in his life reacted to each other in this formal situation.

He stood up and offered his arm, and Freddie slipped hers through it. His cousin had precedence, as he was ostensibly the head of the family because he held the title. Therefore, Abingdon and the dowager countess, then his female cousins, should go first, followed by himself and his future wife, then his mother and whoever cared to bring up the rear.

Instead, Mama charged forward and was about to lead the congregation out. This was a massive breach of etiquette, and he could not allow her to behave so badly. He was about to take action when Freddie squeezed his arm.

'Let it go, Richard. She will regret it herself when she has time to reflect.' He was about to refuse, but she whispered again, 'Please, do it for me, if not for her. It's Christmas Day, a time for goodwill and forgiveness.'

He relaxed and smiled down at her. 'Thank you, sweetheart. That was well done of you. Nobody would have enjoyed a scene.'

The mood in the ballroom was festive, people wishing each other a merry Christmas, eager to begin the celebrations. Richard had expected to find his mother in the dining room as she had left first, but there was no sign of her. No doubt she was embarrassed by her poor behaviour and had retreated to her apartment and would eat there.

By rights, he should serve Freddie and Lucy before helping himself, but the two ladies were already happily filling their plates with coddled eggs, crispy fried ham, and a variety of other items. Breakfast was always generous, but today not only were the usual offerings present, but there was also a variety of freshly baked pastries, pies and pickles. There were the usual silver coffee jugs on the tables, plus porter and also hot spiced wine.

The clatter of cutlery and the raised voices made conversation all but impossible. Richard watched Freddie eat and was pleased she enjoyed her food as much as he did. When they were both done, he suggested they retreat to his study for a while.

She nodded, and they made their way there. He had made sure the fire had been burning for several hours so the room was pleasantly warm.

'We cannot remain here for long,'

Freddie said. 'I heard someone saying you have carol singers from the village coming before it gets dark. Is this a usual thing, or has it been specially arranged because of your house party?'

'It is a family tradition. Whoever comes receives a monetary gift and also food and drink served in the coach house.' He chuckled at her expression of horror. 'Don't worry, sweetheart. The place will be heated with braziers and the refreshments will be hot.'

'At home, most of the staff have Boxing Day free. A cold collation is served by those who prefer to work and receive an extra day in lieu later in the year. They have a party of their own in the servants' hall, and every one of them is given a gift and a gold coin.'

'You can arrange for something similar next year; I'm sure it will be appreciated. We do not exchange gifts at Christmastide but on Twelfth Night. However, as this year we are having a ball, I think this might well be abandoned.'

'That is good news, as my family did not think to bring gifts. Lucy and I receive something on our anniversary, but not at Christmas. By the by, I know nothing about you, which is passing strange as we are engaged to be married.' She curled up on the sofa and tucked her feet beneath her derriere. 'I shall start with something simple. When is your name day?'

He joined her before answering. 'My name day is the first of May.'

'My anniversary and age are already known to you. Why don't we have our nuptials on the second of May? That would mean every year we have two days of celebrations to look forward to.'

'I agree. That way there is no danger of my forgetting the anniversary of our wedding. Your father wishes the ceremony to take place at your house, but Finchley and Abingdon weddings are always held in our own church.'

'Then it is high time you broke with tradition. I shall marry in my own church or not at all.'

She saw him draw breath as if about

to argue, but instead he said something quite unexpected. 'I don't care where it takes place, my love, as long as we do in fact get married.'

'Do you doubt my word? We have agreed we will deal very well together, and I shall not change my mind.'

Then he was on his knees in front of her with the strangest expression on his face. He grasped her hands and raised them to his lips. He kissed each knuckle in turn, sending flickers of pleasure racing around her body.

'I don't know how it has happened, Freddie darling, but I find that despite my best efforts to prevent it, I have fallen irrevocably in love with you. I do not expect you to reciprocate — that was not part of the bargain — but I hope in time you will learn to love me too.'

She was about to reply when the door flew open and his aunt burst into the room. 'Finchley, you must come at once. Your mother has gone. She left me this note.'

He was on his feet and reading it before Freddie had time to catch her breath. She saw his colour fade. 'I shall organise a search party immediately. She must have been out of her mind to have written such a thing.' He glanced in Freddie's direction and smiled sadly. 'Read this; it will explain everything.' He tossed the note in her direction and rushed out.

Dearest sister,
I can remain here no longer. I have no wish to be sent away in disgrace. Finchley has made his choice but I cannot live with that.
I bid you goodbye.

For a moment Freddie was as shocked as Richard had been to think that his poor mother had been driven to end her life by going out into the cold. Then she thought about it. She didn't know a lot about her future mother-in-law, but one thing she was certain of was that she would not take the easy way out of any situation.

This was an attention-seeking ploy — something to draw Richard back to her side and perhaps persuade him to change his mind about the wedding. He would be going on a fool's errand if he ventured outside, and it might be he that lost his life, for Freddie was certain he would not return until he had found his mama.

She must do so first. She doubted anyone had bothered to search the house, as the note had said the silly woman had gone outside. She ran upstairs and headed for the attics — this was where she would go if she wished to remain incognito for an hour or two.

She had the foresight to stop and put on her cloak and collect a candlestick, as she would need both upstairs. This time the door at the top of the steep staircase had not been propped open, and it was difficult negotiating the steps with her skirts over one arm and a candlestick in the other.

She pushed open the door and knew at once she had come to the right place. She could hear the sound of sobbing somewhere in the darkness.

'Mrs Finchley, ma'am, you must not stay up here, for you will catch your death of cold.'

There was a loud, inelegant sniff. 'Go away, you wretched girl. You have ruined my life and the life of my son.'

'Richard is leading a search party outside — do you wish them all to suffer because of your selfishness?'

'He will realise that he has made a disastrous error when he thinks he might have lost his beloved mama because of it. If anything happens to him, it will be your fault, not mine.'

'You are despicable. I love your son and he loves me, and there is nothing you can do to prevent us being happy.'

She was tempted to take away the candlestick, but thought that would be mean-spirited, so carefully placed it on the floor and made her way back downstairs. She had been gone only a few minutes and hoped she would be able to prevent the unnecessary search party from leaving the house.

The sound of raised male voices in the hall added wings to her feet, and she ran to the balustrade. 'Richard, your mother is in the attic. There's no need for you to go outside.'

Her voice carried wonderfully well, and an incredulous hush fell on the assembled company. He was muffled in his greatcoat, lantern in hand, and about to lead the search. He all but threw this at the earl and raced to the stairs.

Freddie hurtled down and inevitably caught her foot in her hem and literally fell into his arms. 'I'm sorry, my love, but your mother is a horrible woman. However, I love you.'

His roar of triumph startled the group into silence a second time, but he ignored them and behaved as if they were quite alone. By the time he released her, they were indeed by themselves in the hall.

'This has proved to be a quite delightful Christmas, my darling lady, and you are the best gift any gentleman could receive.'

We do hope that you have enjoyed reading this large print book.

Did you know that all of our titles are available for purchase?

We publish a wide range of high quality large print books including:
Romances, Mysteries, Classics General Fiction Non Fiction and Westerns

Special interest titles available in large print are:
The Little Oxford Dictionary Music Book, Song Book Hymn Book, Service Book

Also available from us courtesy of Oxford University Press:
Young Readers' Dictionary (large print edition) Young Readers' Thesaurus (large print edition)

For further information or a free brochure, please contact us at:
**Ulverscroft Large Print Books Ltd., The Green, Bradgate Road, Anstey, Leicester, LE7 7FU, England.
Tel:** (00 44) **0116 236 4325
Fax:** (00 44) **0116 234 0205**

GOLDILOCKS WEDDING

Carol MacLean

Goldie Rayner wants her wedding to James to be perfect, and asks her three best friends to help. But April, Rose and Lily have their own problems: April realises that even very self-sufficient people need others sometimes, Rose must deal with the consequences of a break-in at her flat, and Lily is inundated with kittens from an unknown, and unwelcome, benefactor. And as Goldie and James find their differences rising to the surface when emotions run high, is her ex-boyfriend Bryce really the person she should be turning to?

CHRISTMAS AT SPINDLEWOOD

Zara Thorne

Laura Engleby loves Christmas. Her daughter Holly is due home from university, and preparations are in hand for Laura's Christmas Eve party, a tradition started in her late husband's time, to which most of the residents of Charnley Acre are invited. When Clayton Masters, owner of Green and Fragrant Garden Services, finds himself with nowhere to sell his Christmas trees, Laura doesn't hesitate to let him use her garden. But little does she know that the simple act will unleash a winter storm which threatens the future she'd planned for herself.

A RATIONAL PROPOSAL

Jan Jones

When Verity Bowman's uncle dies, she discovers that she's inherited his fortune — as well as his attorney, Charles Congreve. But there's a catch. Concerned that Verity would be tempted to give herself completely to frivolity, her uncle has stipulated that she must first prove to have spent six months 'in a wholly rational manner'. As Charles oversees the conditions of the will, he realises he's falling in love with Verity — but his social position precludes marriage to a wealthy heiress. Can they find a way to make a life together?

BEYOND THE TOUCH OF TIME

Patricia Keyson

A Victorian locket links four stories together, spanning across decades. An aristocrat falls in love with his maid, and heartbreak lies ahead. During World War Two, best friends Barbara and Doreen experience closeness but also jealousy. A young single mother in the 1960s is given the locket, but traumatic events ensue after she casts it aside. And in the present day, Rachel discovers the locket at a car boot sale and wonders about the past of her new talisman, as well as what kind of future it might bring her.

MORE PRECIOUS THAN DIAMONDS

Jean M. Long

Louise Gresham moved to Whitchurch, Kent almost three months ago following a painful break-up with her fiancé. Good fortune landed her a job at Whitchurch Museum, and it is here where she meets handsome thirty-something Nathaniel Prentice. After assisting Nathaniel with his lectures and accompanying him on visits to see his niece, Louise realises she is developing feelings for him. But the past has made her cautious — should she jump straight into another relationship so soon after getting her heart broken?